DOCTOR WHO
THE TIME MONSTER

DOCTOR WHO
THE TIME MONSTER

Based on the BBC television serial by Robert
Sloman by arrangement with the British Broad-
casting Corporation

Terrance Dicks

No. 102
in the
Doctor Who Library

A TARGET BOOK
published by
the Paperback Division of
W. H. ALLEN & Co. PLC

A Target Book
Published in 1986
By the Paperback Division of
W. H. Allen & Co. PLC
44 Hill Street, London W1X 8LB

First published in Great Britain by
W. H. Allen & Co. PLC in 1985

Printed in Great Britain by Anchor Brendon, Tiptree, Essex

The BBC producer of *The Time Monster*
was Barry Letts,
the director was Paul Bernard

ISBN 0 426 20213 9

CONTENTS

1

The Nightmare

The tall, thin man with the young-old face and the mane of prematurely white hair was sleeping uneasily. Suddenly he awoke – to a nightmare.

He was still on the battered leather chaise-longue upon which he had dropped off to sleep – but instead of being in his laboratory he was at the centre of a barren, burning landscape.

All around him volcanoes erupted, sending out streams of burning lava. Lurid jets of flame flared up in smoky dust-laden air.

He sat up – and found himself staring at . . . at what?

A row of strange symbols, looking rather like double headed axes. Suspended before them was a huge, glowing crystal, pulsing with light, shaped like the head of a three-pronged spear, or like Neptune's trident.

Suddenly a sinister black-clad figure loomed up before him.

'Welcome! Welcome to your new Master!'

Volcanoes rumbled, lightning flashed and the figure gave a peal of mocking, triumphant laughter.

More strange and threatening shapes swam up before the dreamer's eyes. Strangely carved statues, demonic face-masks with long, slanting eyes . . .

Suddenly everything erupted in flame. Somewhere, someone was calling him. '*Doctor*! *Doctor*!'

The Doctor awoke, really awoke this time, and found himself back in his laboratory at UNIT HQ. A very small, very pretty fair-haired girl in high boots and a striped woollen mini-dress was shaking his shoulder.

For a moment the Doctor stared at his assistant as if he had no idea who she was. Then he said delightedly, 'Jo! Jo Grant!'

'Are you all right, Doctor?'

'Yes, I think so. I must have been having a nightmare.'

'I'll say you were – a real pippin. Here, I've brought you a cup of tea. Do you want it?'

The Doctor took the cup and saucer. 'Volcanoes . . . earthquakes . . .' Suddenly he leaped up. He handed Jo the untouched cup of tea. 'Thank you, I enjoyed that.'

He wandered over to a lab bench, picked up a small but complicated piece of electronic circuitry and stared absorbedly at it.

'Doctor, have you been working on that thing *all* night again?' asked Jo accusingly. 'What is it anyway – a super dematerialisation circuit?'

(At this time in his lives, the Doctor, now in his third incarnation, had been exiled to Earth by his Time Lord superiors. The TARDIS, his space-time machine, no longer worked properly. Much of his time was spent in an attempt to get it working again, and resume his wanderings through time and space.)

'No, no, the dematerialisation circuit will have to wait. This is something far more imporant. It might make all the difference the next time *he* turns up.'

'The next time who turns up?'

2

'The Master, of course.'

The Master, like the Doctor, was a sort of renegade Time Lord, though of a very different kind. The Doctor's wanderings through the cosmos were a result of simple curiosity. Such interventions as he made in the affairs of the planets he visited were motivated always by his concern to defeat evil and assist good.

The Master, on the other hand, was dedicated to evil; *his* schemes had always had conquest and self-aggrandisement as their goals.

Once good friends, the Doctor and the Master had long been deadly enemies. The Master's sudden arrival on the planet Earth had led to a resumption of the long-standing feud between them.

The Master's desire to defeat and destroy the Doctor, preferably in the most agonising and humiliating fashion possible, was quite as strong as his desire to rule the Universe.

And the Master had been part of the Doctor's nightmare . . . Perhaps the Doctor's subconscious mind, or that now-dormant telepathic facility that was part of his Time Lord make-up, was attempting to deliver some kind of warning. Perhaps he had somehow picked up a hint of the Master's latest, and no doubt diabolical, scheme . . .

The Doctor swung round. 'Now Jo, listen carefully. I want you to go and find out, as quickly as you can, if there have been any volcanic eruptions or severe earthquakes recently – anywhere in the world.'

'You're joking of course!'

'Believe me, Jo, this is no joking matter.'

'But I read it all out to you last night,' said Jo indignantly. 'It just shows, you never listen to a word

I say.' She went over to a side table, picked up a folded copy of *The Times* and perched on the edge of the Doctor's desk. 'Here we are. New eruptions in the Thera group of islands, somewhere off Greece.'

'Does it say anything about a crystal?'

'What crystal? Look, Doctor, I know I'm exceedingly dim, but please explain.'

'It was in my dream,' said the Doctor slowly. 'A big crystal, shaped something like a trident . . .'

Not far away, in his attic laboratory at the Newton Institute, Professor Thascalos held a trident-shaped crystal aloft. 'Observe – a simple piece of quartz, nothing more.'

Carefully he fitted the crystal into the centre of a cabinet packed with electronic equipment. He placed a transparent protective cover over the apparatus and stepped back.

He was a medium-sized, compactly but powerfully built man, this Professor Thascalos, with sallow skin and a neatly-trimmed pointed beard. His dark burning eyes radiated energy and power.

Beside him stood his assistant, Doctor Ruth Ingram, an attractive looking woman with short fair hair and an air of brisk no-nonsense efficiency about her. Like the Professor, she wore a crisp white lab coat.

She looked exasperatedly at her superior. 'But that's ridiculous!'

'Of course it is, Doctor Ingram,' agreed the Professor. His deep voice had just the faintest tinge of a Greek accent. 'Of course it is. There is no way for me to prove to you that this crystal is different from any other piece of quartz, yet it is unique. As you say, ridiculous!'

4

They were standing in the small inner section of the lab, divided from the rest of the lab by a protective wall of specially strengthened glass.

Slipping off his lab coat to reveal a beautifully tailored dark suit, the Professor moved through into the main laboratory. Like the smaller one, it held an astonishing variety of electronic equipment, crammed into what had once been servants' quarters in a great country house.

Ruth Ingram followed him. 'And this crystal is the missing piece of equipment we've been waiting for?'

'Exactly!'

Suddenly the door burst open and a tall, gangling young man rushed in, managing in the process to fall over his own feet.

'I swear I switch that alarm off in my sleep!' He had a shock of untidy brown hair and a long straggly moustache – intended to make him look more mature – gave him instead a faintly comic air.

At the sight of the Professor he skidded to a halt. 'Oops! Sorry, Prof.'

Stuart Hyde was the third member of the Professor's little research team, a post-graduate student working for a higher degree.

'Simmer down, Stu, for Pete's sake,' said Ruth. But she couldn't help smiling. There was something endearingly puppyish about Stuart Hyde.

The Professor however was not amused. 'Don't call me Prof!'

Stuart groaned. 'In the dog house again!'

The Professor glanced at his watch. 'Be quiet and listen to me. I have been summoned to a meeting with our new Director in exactly two and a half minutes. I shall have to leave the final checks for the demonstration to the pair of you.'

Ruth was both astonished and alarmed. 'Aren't we going to have a trial run first?'

The experimental apparatus on which they had all been working was due to be demonstrated to one of the Institute's directors that very morning – a director who also happened to be Chairman of the Grants Committee.

The Professor shook his head decisively. 'A trial run? It's not necessary, my dear.'

'That's marvellous,' said Stuart gloomily. 'We're going to look a right bunch of Charlies if something goes wrong when this fellow from the Grants Committee turns up. We'll be left there with egg on our faces.'

'Surely, Professor –' began Ruth.

'Now, now, my dear, there's no need for you to worry your pretty little head.'

He could scarcely have said anything calculated to annoy Ruth Ingram more. 'And there's no need for you to be so insufferably patronising, Professor. Just because I'm a woman . . .'

Stuart sighed. 'Here we go again!'

The Professor said instantly, 'You're quite right, Doctor Ingram. Please, forgive me.' He paused in the doorway. 'Now, will you be so good as to run those checks?'

The door closed behind him.

Ruth stood staring furiously at it. 'That man! I don't know which infuriates me more, his dictatorial attitude or that infernal courtesy of his!' She sighed. 'It's all the same really – a bland assumption of male superiority!'

Stuart grinned. 'May God bless the good ship Women's Lib and all who sail in her.'

Privately however, Stuart was thinking that Ruth

6

had got it wrong. The Professor didn't assume that he was superior just to women.

He was superior to everybody.

Mike Yates spread out the map of the Mediterranean on the Doctor's table and pointed. 'There you are, Jo, the Thera group. Those little islands there.'

Jo looked up at the Doctor who was busy at his lab bench. 'Doctor, come and look!'

'Not now, Jo, I'm busy.'

'But it's that map you asked for.'

A little grumpily the Doctor put down his circuit. 'Oh, I see!' He wandered over and looked at the map. 'Mmm, Thera . . .'

Jo waited expectantly.

'Doesn't mean a thing to me!' The Doctor returned to his bench.

Jo peered at the map. 'It says "Santorini" in brackets. Must be another name for it. What about that?'

The Doctor was immersed in his work. 'Forget it, Jo. I had a nightmare, that's all.'

Jo gave Mike Yates an apologetic look. 'Sorry, Mike.'

He began rolling up the map. 'Not to worry! Better than hanging about the Duty Room. If nothing turns up soon I'll go round the twist.'

'That makes two of us. And here I was thinking we were going off on a trip to Atlantis.'

The Doctor swung round. '*What*?'

'I was just saying to Mike.'

'You said *Atlantis*,' interrupted the Doctor. 'Why Atlantis?'

'Well, it said so in the paper, didn't it?'

The Doctor strode over to them. 'The map, Captain Yates, the map!'

Hurriedly Mike began unrolling the map again.

Jo picked up the newspaper. 'Here it is . . . "Believed by many modern historians to be all that remains of Plato's Metropolis of Atlantis".'

The Doctor brooded over the map. 'Of course, of course . . .'

Mike looked puzzled. 'Atlantis? I thought it was supposed to be in the middle of the Atlantic Ocean?'

Jo was studying the article. 'You're out of date. Apparently it was part of the Minoan civilisation – you know, the Minotaur and all that.'

'It's only legends though, isn't it?'

The Doctor straightened up. 'Get me the Brigadier on the telephone, will you Jo?'

'What, now?'

'Yes, *now*,' snapped the Doctor.

Jo leaped up. 'Sorry!' She reached for the phone.

Mike watched her dial. 'The Brig? Why the Brig, for heaven's sake?'

'Search me!' Jo listened for a second, then handed the phone to the Doctor. 'The Brigadier!'

The Doctor snatched the receiver. 'Brigadier? Now listen to me! I want you to put out a world-wide warning. Alert all your precious UNIT HQs. Not that it'll do any good!'

On the other end of the line, Brigadier Alastair Lethbridge-Stewart, Commanding Officer of the British section of the United Nations Intelligence Taskforce, stroked his neatly-trimmed military moustache. 'Thank you very much, Doctor. And against what, precisely, am I supposed to be warning the world?'

'The Master. I've just seen him.'

8

'You've seen him? Where? When?' The Brigadier leaped to his feet. 'Never mind. Stay right where you are Doctor. I'll be with you in a jiffy.'

A few minutes later, the Brigadier was bursting into the Doctor's laboratory. 'Now then, Doctor, you said you'd seen the Master? Where? When?'

The Doctor looked a little sheepish. 'In a dream. Not half an hour ago.'

The Brigadier sank down onto a stool. 'I can hardly put UNIT on full alert on the strength of your dreams, Doctor. In any case, *every* section of UNIT now has the search for the Master written into its standing orders.'

'Priority Z-44, I suppose.'

'Priority A-1, actually.'

'I tell you Brigadier, there is grave danger.'

'Danger of what for heaven's sake?'

'I'm not sure,' said the Doctor tetchily. 'But I tell you I saw danger quite clearly in my dream.'

'A *dream*! If that got out I'd be the laughing-stock of UNIT. Really, Doctor, you'll be consulting the entrails of a sheep next.'

Jo giggled.

The Brigadier glared reprovingly at her and went on, 'Right now, we'd better be on our way to the Newton Institute. Are you ready, Doctor?'

'Certainly not, Brigadier. I'm far too busy to go anywhere.'

'But I told them you'd go. They're expecting two observers from UNIT.'

The Doctor picked up his circuit and went on with his work.

'Shall I go?' asked Jo brightly.

'Certainly not,' snapped the Doctor. 'I need you here.'

Jo turned to the Brigadier. 'What's it all about anyway?'

'TOMTIT, that's what it's about, Miss Grant. A demonstration of TOMTIT.'

'TOMTIT? What on earth does that stand for?' asked Mike.

The Brigadier cleared his throat. 'Well, er . . .'

The Doctor spoke without looking up. 'Transmission Of Matter Through Interstitial Time.'

'Exactly,' said the Brigadier. 'TOMTIT.'

Jo was none the wiser. 'But what does it *do*?'

Here the Brigadier was on firmer ground. 'Brilliant idea. It can actually break down solid objects into light waves or whatever, and transmit them from one place to another.'

'And it *works*?' asked Yates incredulously.

The Brigadier shrugged. 'Apparently. Well, Yates, you'd better come with me, I suppose.'

'Sorry sir,' said Mike a little smugly. 'I'm Duty Officer.'

Unable to contravene his own orders, the Brigadier looked round helplessly. 'Well, someone's got to come with me . . .'

The door opened and a brawny young man in civvies marched in, carrying a weekend bag. 'Just off, sir.'

The Brigadier beamed. 'Sergeant Benton. The very man!'

Sergeant Benton saw trouble coming, and tried vainly to dodge. 'I was just leaving, sir. 48 hour pass.'

'Oh no you're not, Sergeant. You're coming with me on a little trip to the Newton Institute.'

10

'Yessir,' said Benton resignedly. 'The what, sir?'

'The Newton Institute. Research establishment at Wootton, just outside Cambridge . . .'

'Charlatan?' snarled Professor Thascalos. 'How dare you call *me* a charlatan, Doctor Perceval!' His dark eyes seemed to blaze with fury.

The portly silver-haired man on the other side of the desk winced before the Professor's fury, but he stood his ground. 'Doctor Cook is not only Chairman of the Grants Committee, but a colleague and a personal friend of mine. Am I to tell him this afternoon that I am as gullible as that drunkard I have replaced?'

The Professor smiled grimly and made no reply. Doctor Perceval's predecessor had indeed been over-fond of the bottle, an easy man to impress and to deceive.

Doctor Perceval however was a far more sceptical character. 'How is it that I can find no trace of your academic career, *before* your brief visit to Athens University? How is it that you have published nothing, that you refuse even to discuss the hypothesis behind your so-called experiments, that the very name of your project is arrant nonsense? TOMTIT! What, pray, is Interstitial Time?'

The one who called himself Professor Thascalos leaned forward, hands on the desk, staring into the new director's eyes. 'You're a very clever man, Director. I can see that I shall have to tell you everything. You're quite right of course, I am no Professor.'

'Ah!' said the Director triumphantly.

The mellow voice said soothingly. 'I can see that you are disturbed but you have nothing to worry

11

about. You must believe me . . . you *must* believe me . . .'

The dark eyes seemed to burn into the Director's brain, the deep voice vibrated inside his skull. He swayed a little on his feet.

'Must believe you,' he muttered. 'I must believe you.'

The deep voice rose to a triumphant crescendo. 'I am the Master. You will listen to me – and you will obey me. *You will obey me!*'

2

The Test

Suddenly the Director found that everything had become very clear. There was no problem, no reason for concern. It was very simple. All he needed to do was to obey. Indeed the very word vibrated inside his brain. '*Obey . . . obey . . . obey . . .* '

'That's better,' said the Master gently. 'Now, you just sit there quietly and await the arrival of this wretched man from London. And remember – you are perfectly satisfied as to the integrity of my work here and the authenticity of my credentials. You understand?'

The Director sank slowly back into his chair. 'Yes . . . I understand.'

In the laboratory, now filled with the high pitched oscillating whine of the TOMTIT apparatus, Ruth was checking readings on an instrument console. She was using an intercom to call the results through to Stuart, who was crouched over a complex piece of apparatus in the inner lab.

'One point three five nine,' she called.

Stuart's voice came faintly back. 'One point three five nine – check.'

'Two point zero four five.'

'Two point zero four five – check.'

'Three point zero six two.'

'Three point zero six two. Check.'

'Fifty-nine and steady.'

'Fifty nine and steady – check.'

Ruth flicked switches and the noise died away. 'And that's the lot.'

'And that's the lot – check, check, check!' parroted Stuart. He came through from the inner laboratory.

'And now we just sit and wait,' said Ruth disgustedly. 'I still think it's just plain stupid not to have a trial run. Ludicrous!'

'Ludicrous, check!'

'Oh, grow up, Stu!'

'No, but I mean it, love, it *is* ludicrous. Just suppose this thing won't wag its tail when we tell it to?'

'They'd withdraw the grant.'

'As sure as God made little green apples. And bang goes my fellowship.'

'Bang goes my job,' said Ruth. '*And* my scientific reputation for that matter.' She snorted. 'Men! It's their conceit that bugs me.'

'Hey, hey, hey,' protested Stuart. 'I'm on your side, remember?'

'Oh well, you don't count!'

'Oh, do't I?'

'Don't bully me, Stu, or I think I'll burst into tears.'

There was a moment of gloomy silence. Then Stuart looked up. 'Let's do it!'

'What?'

'Have a run-through.'

Ruth looked instinctively at the door. 'Without – *him*?'

'Why not?'

'Well, it's the Professor's project after all,' said Ruth doubtfully. 'He *is* the boss.'

'Nominally, perhaps. But when you think how much you've put into it, Ruth, it becomes a joint affair. You've as much right to take that sort of decision as he has.'

Ruth was tempted but uncertain. 'Well . . .'

Stuart played his ace. 'Of course, if you feel you *need* to have a man in charge . . .'

'That does it. We go ahead.'

'That's my girl!'

Ruth gave him an exasperated look and went over to the controls.

Jo Grant looked furiously at the Doctor who was still hard at work on his complex piece of circuitry. He was fitting it into a carrying case which was shaped rather like a table tennis bat. The rounded end held dials and a little rotating aerial.

'You know, Doctor,' said Jo conversationally, 'you're quite the most annoying person I've ever met. I've asked you at least a million times. What *is* that thing?'

The Doctor looked absently at her. 'Extraordinary. I could have sworn I'd told you . . . It's a time sensor, Jo.'

'I see.'

'Do you? What does it do then?'

'Well, it . . . it's a . . . Obviously it detects disturbances in the Time Field.'

The Doctor gave her an admiring look. 'Very good. You're learning, Jo. Yes, this is just what you need if you happen to be looking for a TARDIS.'

'It's a TARDIS sniffer-outer!'

'Precisely. Or any other time-machine for that matter. So, if the Master does turn up . . .'

'Bingo!'

'As you so rightly say, Jo – Bingo!'

Stuart was laboriously climbing into an all-enveloping protective suit which made him look like a rather comic astronaut. 'I feel like the back end of a pantomime horse.'

'Very suitable for a keen young man like you,' said Ruth briskly.

'Come again?'

'Starting at the bottom!'

Stuart groaned. 'Anyway, it's all a waste of time. Why should there be any radiation danger at the receiver? We're only going to use about ten degrees.'

'Are you willing to take the risk?'

Stuart thought for a moment. 'No!'

'Then stop beefing and get on with it!'

Fitting the visored helmet over his head, Stuart went through into the inner section of the laboratory – the receiving area.

Ruth operated controls and the TOMTIT noise began, rising steadily in pitch and volume . . .

(Blissfully unaware of all this scientific activity, the Institute's regular window cleaner was setting his ladder up against the laboratory window. He peered curiously at the radiation suited figure in the lab, then reached for his wash-leather.)

Ruth went to a shelf and took down a white marble vase. It had curved sides and a domed lid, and looked rather like a giant chess pawn.

She put the case on a flat surface beneath a complex looking focussing device, then returned to her control panel.

Stuart's voice came from the intercom. 'Interstitial activity – nil.'

Ruth checked the dial on her console. 'Molecular structure, stable. Increasing power.'

The oscillating whine of TOMTIT rose higher. In the inner lab the crystal began to glow.

With the Doctor's time sensor in her hand, Jo stood looking apprehensively at the open door of the TARDIS, which was making a strange wheezing, groaning sound. 'I say, Doctor, you're not going to disappear to Venus or somewhere?'

The Doctor's voice came through the TARDIS door. 'No, of course not. Just keep your eyes on those dials!'

Suddenly the dials began flickering wildly, the aerial spun frantically, and the device gave out a high pitched bleeping sound.

'It's working!' said Jo excitedly.

'Of course it is. Make a note of the readings will you?'

Jo grabbed a note pad and pencil.

Ruth was still calling out the readings. 'Thirty-five . . . forty . . . forty-five . . .'

Stuart's voice came back. 'Check, check, check.'

'Increasing power . . .'

The circular aerial on top of the Doctor's device was revolving wildly. It slowed and stopped as the TARDIS noise died away.

The Doctor came marching out, took the note pad with the readings from Jo's hand and began studying it absorbedly.

'Well done,' said Jo.

17

'Thank you,' said the Doctor modestly.

'It's a bit out on distance though. Says the TARDIS is only three feet away.'

'Those are Venusian feet,' said the Doctor solemnly.

'I see. They're larger than ours?'

'Oh yes, much larger, Jo. The Venusians are always tripping over themselves.'

Suddenly the time sensor came to life again. Jo jumped, 'You must have left something switched on in the TARDIS, Doctor.'

'I most certainly did not. Why?'

Jo handed him the sensor. 'Look, it's working again. And the readings are different.'

The Doctor stared indignantly at the sensor. 'That's impossible – unless . . .'

'Unless what?'

The Doctor said slowly, 'Unless someone's operating another TARDIS.'

In the inner laboratory Ruth's voice came to Stuart over the intercom. 'Isolate matrix scanner.'

Stuart reached for a control with his gloved hand. 'Check.' In front of Stuart there was a square metal platform with a focussing device suspended over it – the exact duplicate of the one before Ruth in the outer lab.

Suddenly on that platform there appeared the ghostly outline of a vase.

'It's going to work!' shouted Stuart excitedly.

Ruth's calm voice came back. 'Pipe down and concentrate. Stand by. Initiating transfer.'

Stuart began the countdown. 'Ten . . . nine . . . eight . . .'

The crystal glowed brighter.

18

In the Director's study the Master had installed himself at the Director's desk, calmly drafting a proposal to double his own grant for the Director to sign. The clock of what had once been the old stables began to chime. Suddenly the Master frowned and looked up. The chiming was slow, dragging, slurred, as if the old clock was somehow running down. But the Master knew better. It wasn't the clock that was slowing down – it was time itself.

'*The fools!*' he snarled, and hurried from the room.

'Four . . . three . . . two . . . one!' chanted Stuart.

In the outer lab the vase became transparent, then faded slowly away . . .

. . . to re-appear, solid and real on the receiving plate in front of Stuart.

Rapidly he operated controls. 'Transfer stabilising. Okay Ruth, switch off. We've done it!'

He expected the noise of TOMTIT to die away, but it didn't. The oscilliating whine rose higher.

He heard Ruth's voice over the intercom. 'Stuart, come here. There's a positive feedback. She's overloading!'

Pulling off his helmet, Stuart rushed back to the outer lab where he found Ruth busy at her console.

Without looking up she said, 'You'll have to bring the surge down as I reduce the power or she'll blow.'

Stuart ran to the console. 'Right.'

The astonished window cleaner was still perched at the top of his ladder, staring at the glowing crystal as if hypnotised. Suddenly a giant surge of power struck him, like a push from an invisible hand.

He flew backwards off his ladder, and *floated* rather than fell to the ground below.

The Master, crossing the courtyard observed this phenomenon without surprise. He hurried towards the door that led to the laboratory.

As he came closer, he leaned forward against the thrust of some invisible resistance, like a man walking against a high wind.

The stable clock was still giving out its low, dragging chime.

In the laboratory itself, the calm centre of this localised temporal storm, things seemed normal enough.

Ruth and Stuart were in the inner lab examining the vase on its metal platform. The crystal was still glowing brightly.

Carefully, Stuart lifted the vase from its platform. 'It looks fine!'

Ruth nodded. 'Be careful. Bring it through here.' She led the way back into the main lab.

Carefully, Stuart stood the vase on a bench. 'I don't believe it. We've really done it!'

'It'll have to be checked for any structural changes,' said Ruth cautiously.

'OH, FOR Pete's sake,' said Stuart explosively, 'it's as good as new, you can see it is.' He grabbed her by the shoulders and began waltzing her round the room to a triumphant chant of 'We've done it, we've done it, we've done it!'

The dance stopped abruptly as they waltzed straight into the Master. He was standing in the doorway, an angry scowl on his face.

The Doctor was studying a map. 'I'd place it in that

segment there, Jo. Anything from fifty to a hundred miles from here.'

'Not much to go on.'

'Not unless he switches his TARDIS on again . . .'

Jo looked hopefully at him. 'Well, you never know. He might.'

'And in that case Jo, if we were a bit nearer, and in Bessie . . .'

'Right,' said Jo. 'Come on then, Doctor, let's go. You bring the map.'

The Master was in a towering rage. 'You are a fool, Doctor Ingram.'

Ruth felt herself quailing beneath the sheer force of his anger, which made her all the more determined to stand up for herself. 'You have no right to talk to me like that, Professor.'

'Be silent! You might have caused irreparable damage.'

'I was in full control the whole time. If you have no confidence in me –'

The Master cut across her. 'That is quite irrelevant. Mr Hyde, why did *you* allow this stupidity?'

'Hang about,' protested Stuart. 'I'm not my sister's keeper, you know. She's the boss.' He hesitated and then admitted, 'In any case, I was the one who suggested it.'

The Master turned away. 'I might have known. Just like an irresponsible schoolboy. You'll pay for this!'

Ruth came to the defence of her colleague. 'The decision was entirely mine, Professor. I take full responsibility for testing the apparatus, and I'm prepared to justify my action at the highest level.

Perhaps we had better go and see the Director and sort all this out before the demonstration.'

With a mighty effort the Master controlled himself. When he spoke, his voice was once again calm and reasonable. 'I'm sorry Doctor Ingram, you must excuse me. It will not be necessary to take this matter any further.'

But now Ruth was angry in her turn. 'That's all very well, Professor. After the things you've been saying –'

'Please,' said the Master forcefully. 'Accept my apologies.'

Ruth drew a deep breath. 'Well, perhaps it was a bit unethical of me not to have told you.'

'Come off it, Ruth,' said Stuart. 'He's only climbing down because he needs you for the demonstration.'

'How very clever of you, Mr Hyde,' said the Master smoothly. 'Of course I need you, both of you.'

Stuart couldn't help feeling mollified. 'After all Prof, let's face it, we couldn't risk a foul-up this afternoon, could we?'

'Say no more,' said the Master magnanimously. 'The matter is closed.'

'Well, not quite,' said Ruth a little guiltily. 'You see, it wasn't all plain sailing. We had some sort of positive feedback. There was an overload.'

'But that's impossible.'

'See for yourself.' She tore off the print-out from the computer and handed it to him.

The Master studied it thoughtfully. 'I see . . . Of course, how foolish of me.'

They heard Stuart calling from the inner lab. 'Hey, Ruth, Professor. The crystal – it's still glowing!'

The Master snapped his fingers. 'Of course it is! I see . . .'

Ruth looked dubiously at him. 'You know what caused the overload then?'

'Of course. You must have been drawing some kind of power from outside time itself. We must build a time vector filter into the transmitter.' The Master snatched up a pencil from the bench, and began drawing on the computer read-out paper. 'Here, let me show you.' With amazing speed, he sketched an elaborate circuit diagram. 'You see? In effect, it's a sort of paracybernetic control circuit.'

Ruth studied the diagram. 'Yes, I see. But won't this take some time to line up? The demonstration is at two.'

'Indeed it will – and I'm afraid I must leave the task to you. I am expected to eat a pretentious lunch and exchange banalities with our guests.'

Stuart Hyde was an amiable soul and he was happy that a semblance of good feeling had been restored. 'Don't worry, Prof, you go off and enjoy your nosh. Leave it to the toiling masses.'

'I have every confidence in you, Mr Hyde.' said the Master smoothly. 'And of course, in you, Doctor Ingram.'

Stuart had wandered over to the window. 'Hey, you'd better get your skates on, Professor. The VIPs are arriving . . . escorted by UNIT no less.'

The Master hurried to the window.

An enormous black limousine was gliding up the drive, with an Army landrover close behind it. Gold letters were painted on the side panel of the jeep.

'UNIT,' muttered the Master. 'What are *they* doing here?'

Stuart shrugged. 'Military observers, I suppose.

23

Happens all the time. The Government are the only people with the money for our sort of nonsense these days.'

The Master turned away from the window. 'Doctor Ingram I have changed my mind. *I* shall stay here and set up the time vector filter myself – with the assistance of Mr Hyde, of course.'

Ruth gave him an offended look. 'I assure you I am perfectly capable of constructing the circuit –'

'And I am sure you are equally capable of eating a tough pheasant on my behalf.'

'But why don't you want to go suddenly?'

The Master's voice was throbbing with sincerity. 'I am a life-long pacifist, Doctor Ingram. The association of the military, with violence, with killing . . .'He shuddered delicately. 'Please bear with me.'

Ruth thought the Professor made a most unlikely pacifist, but she had no alternative but to agree. 'Very well. I'll get them to send you some sandwiches across.'

'Good thinking, Batman,' said Stuart. As he helped her off with her lab coat he whispered, 'We've got a right nutcase on our hands!'

3

The Summoning

The occupants of the two vehicles parked outside the Institute were staring in astonishment at what looked like a freak accident. They stood in a little semi-circle around the window cleaner who was laying sprawled out and motionless on the gravel drive.

There were four of them in the group: Doctor Cook, chairman of the Grants Committee, a serious, indeed pompous man in his middle fifties; Proctor his assistant, younger, and nervously deferential; Sergeant Benton, back in uniform and still sighing for his vanished leave; and finally, there was the immaculate figure of Brigadier Lethbridge-Stewart, who was kneeling beside the body and taking its pulse.

'He's not dead, is he?' asked Doctor Cook nervously.

The Brigadier stood up. 'No, he's still breathing.'

'Well – who is he?'

The Brigadier glanced at the ladder still propped up against the building. 'A window cleaner, I presume. Must have fallen off his ladder.' He studied the unconscious but apparently uninjured form. 'It's a miracle he's still alive.'

'Poor fellow,' said Cook indifferently. 'Come

along, Proctor. I trust you'll make the necessary arrangements to get the man to hospital, Brigadier?'

The Brigadier too knew all about the advantages of delegation. 'Yes, of course sir, leave it to me.' He raised his voice. 'Sergeant Benton! See to it will you?'

Bessie, the Doctor's little yellow roadster, shot along the narrow country lane with the Doctor at the wheel. He cut a colourful figure in his elegant burgundy smoking jacket, ruffled shirt and flowing cloak. Beside him sat Jo Grant, a map spread out on her lap, the time sensor resting on top of it. She was wearing a warm fluffy coat over her mini-dress.

She glanced up at the sky which was dull and overcast. 'Isn't it a doomy day? I mean, look at that sky. Just *look* at it!'

The Doctor was concentrating on his driving. 'My dear girl, stop whiffling. We're not out on a pleasure jaunt.'

'Sorry, Doctor.'

What they were out on, thought Jo, was more of a wild goose chase. The plan was to drive about in a more or less random search pattern, covering the general area from which the mysterious time signal had originated.

The Doctor said, 'If it is the Master, we can't run the risk of losing him. So you just keep your eye on the sensor.'

Obediently Jo glanced at the sensor on her lap and found to her astonishment that its little scanner aerial was whirling frantically.

'Doctor, it's working again!'

The Doctor stopped the car. 'What's the bearing?'

Jo made a rapid calculation. 'Zero seven four. And it's . . . sixteen point thirty-nine miles away.'

'That's Venusian miles. That'd be seventy-two point seventy-eight miles . . .' He studied the map. 'Which puts it about – *here*. A village called Wootton.'

'Wootton? But that's where the Brigadier and Sergeant Benton went to.'

'TOMTIT!' said the Doctor. 'If the Master's behind that . . . What time's the demonstration, Jo?'

'Two o'clock, I think.'

'We've got to stop it!'

The Doctor started the car, and flicked the super-drive switch. Bessie streaked away at an impossibly high speed.

Ruth Ingram was thoroughly relieved when lunch was over at last. It *had* been pheasant – tough pheasant – just as the Professor had predicted.

Socially speaking, it had not been the most enjoyable of occasions. Throughout the meal, Doctor Cook had whinged on about the need for stringent economies. Indeed, he was still doing so now as the little group made its way into the TOMTIT laboratory.

'Well, that's how it is, Charles. It may seem churlish of me after eating your excellent lunch – though how the Institute can afford pheasant I really don't know . . .'

'We *are* in the depths of the country,' protested the Director feebly. He had been silent and abstracted throughout the meal as if part of his mind wasn't really with them at all.

Cook strode on into the laboratory. 'Be that as it may, we are responsible for international funds, public money. I doubt very much whether we should allow ourselves the luxury of either pheasants *or* TOMTITs.' He laughed loudly at his own laborious joke, and Proctor tittered obsequiously.

Ruth looked round the empty laboratory. 'Well,' she said awkwardly, 'the Professor doesn't seem to be here.'

'Obviously,' said the Director pettishly.

Stuart came from the inner laboratory, suited up except for his helmet, which he carried under one arm.

Ruth greeted him with relief. 'There you are, Stuart. Where's the Professor?'

'Search me. He was here a couple of minutes ago.'

'Who is this fellow Thascalos, anyway?' demanded Cook. 'I've never heard of him.'

The Director seemed to come to life. 'Oh, an excellent background, excellent,' he said enthusiastically. 'Surely you've read his paper on the granular structure of time?'

'It's all I can do to keep up with my Departmental papers,' said Cook loftily. 'I leave all the rest to Proctor here.'

He glanced sharply at his assistant, who shook his head apologetically. 'New one on me, sir, I'm afraid.'

The Brigadier was gazing around the laboratory which was cluttered with equipment. 'Fearsome looking load of electronic nonsense you've got here, Doctor Ingram,' he said briskly. 'How does it work – and what does it do?'

Ruth drew a deep breath. 'Well . . .'

'In words of one syllable, please,' said the Brigadier hurriedly.

Ruth smiled. 'I'll do my best. Now, according to

28

Professor Thascalos's theory, time isn't smooth. It's made up of bits.'

'A series of minute present-moments,' said Stuart helpfully.

Ruth nodded. 'That's it. Temporal atoms, so to speak. So, if one could push something through the interstices between them, it would be outside our space-time continuum altogether.'

The Brigadier gave her a baffled look. 'Where would it be, then?'

'Nowhere at all, in ordinary terms.'

'You've lost me, Doctor Ingram.'

'And me,' said Humphrey Cook emphatically. 'Never heard such a farrago of unscientific rubbish in my life. It's an impossible concept.'

'But we've done it,' said Stuart triumphantly. 'We shoved a vase through here –' He indicated the transmission platform – 'and brought it back in there.' And he pointed to the inner laboratory.

'Shoved it through where?' asked the Brigadier exasperatedly.

Benton, who had been standing silent and a little overawed at the back of the group said unexpectedly, 'Through the crack between now and now, sir.'

The Brigadier shook his head. Where was the Doctor when he needed him? 'I give up. It's beyond me.'

A deep, foreign-accented voice said, 'Then you must see for yourselves!'

In the doorway stood a figure in a radiation suit, features obscured by the visored helmet. 'I must apologise for keeping you all waiting. Shall we begin?'

29

Jo clutched the edge of her seat as Bessie sped along the lanes at a speed, she was sure, of several hundred miles an hour. 'Please slow down, Doctor. It's not safe to drive so quickly.' They were moving so fast that the countryside around them was no more than a blur.

'It's perfectly safe,' shouted the Doctor cheerfully. 'My reactions are ten times as fast as yours, remember. And Bessie's no ordinary car.'

They were streaking along a comparatively straight stretch of road when, to her horror, Jo saw that a main highway was cutting across it at right angles.

They swept up to the junction, the Doctor's foot pressed steadily on the brake, and Bessie stopped – instantly.

Jo gulped. 'Why didn't I go through the windscreen?'

'Because Bessie's brakes work by the absorption of inertia – including yours.'

Suddenly Jo's attention was caught by the whirring of the time sensor. 'It's starting again!'

'Come on, Bessie, old girl,' said the Doctor. 'It's up to you!'

Checking that the junction was clear, the Doctor started Bessie up again and shot off even faster than before.

Unfortunately it was a case of more haste, less speed. Just beyond the junction was the notice board signalling the way to the Newton Institute. The Doctor and Jo shot straight past without even seeing it . . .

In the TOMTIT laboratory, the Master switched on the power. The experiment was about to begin.

'Surely you don't need to wear radiation gear out here, Professor?' asked Ruth.

'A precaution in case of emergency, my dear. I may have to join Mr Hyde in the inner laboratory in a hurry.' He leaned over the intercom. 'Report!'

Stuart's voice came from the speaker. 'Interstitial activity, nil.'

Ruth was placing a rather handsome cup and saucer on the metal transmitting platform. She checked a dial. 'Molecular structure stable.'

'Increasing power,' snapped the Master.

The oscillating whine of TOMTIT rose higher.

Ruth's voice was tense. 'Isolate matrix scanner.'

'Check'

'Increasing power,' said the Master again.

Ruth gave him a worried look. 'But you're into the second quadrant already, Professor.'

'*I know what I'm doing.*' The Master spoke more calmly. 'Initiating transfer!'

He threw a switch and to the astonishment of the Brigadier and the other onlookers, the cup and saucer faded slowly away.

'Good heavens,' said the Brigadier. He looked through the partition and saw the cup and saucer standing on the receiving platform in the inner laboratory, the radiation-suited figure of Stuart Hyde hovering over it.

Suddenly Stuart's voice crackled frantically from the intercom. 'I'm getting too much power again. I can't hold it. Switch off. Switch off!'

Ruth turned to the Professor, and was horrified to see that he was actually increasing the power. 'Turn it off!' she shouted.

But the figure at the controls seemed rapt, enchanted.

31

Throwing back his head the Master roared, 'Come, Kronos – *come*! I summon you!'

4

The Ageing

In the inner laboratory the crystal glowed with a fierce, almost unbearable brightness.

Even through the darkened vision-plate of Stuart's helmet it's intensity was dazzling. He staggered back . . .

Suddenly the transferred cup and saucer glowed brightly, then shattered.

In their place Stuart sensed rather than saw something else beginning to form.

A winged shape . . .

A tendril of fire snaked out, groping aimlessly. It touched Stuart, and his whole body glowed brightly for a second.

He staggered back, clawed at his helmet and collapsed. Beneath the helmet, his face began to change . . .

Ruth saw him fall, and ran to the partition door. She was about to go to his assistance then stopped herself. The radiation level in the inner lab was still dangerously high. But Professor Thascalos was already suited up.

She swung round and called 'Professor!' To her horror, she saw that the Professor had disappeared.

Ruth ran back to the main control console. Stuart

would have to wait. The essential thing now was to turn off the power – if she could . . .

It didn't take the Doctor long to realise that he had overshot his destination. He stopped the car, studied the map and swung the car in a U-turn. Minutes later he was streaking up the drive of the Newton Institute and making one of his amazing stops before the main door.

The Doctor jumped out of the car. 'Right, Jo . . . Oh, good grief!'

Jo Grant didn't move or speak. She was sitting quite still, staring straight ahead of her.

For a moment the Doctor thought she must be stunned by the speed of the journey. The he realised that it was something else entirely that was happening – something that confirmed his worst fears. Someone was interfering with time.

As he turned away from the car, he felt the resistance of the temporal disturbance. Forcing his way through it, the Doctor used the resistance as a guide, letting it lead him to its source. He ran through the archway at the side of the main building, across the courtyard beyond, through the white-painted door on the other side.

In his haste, the Doctor failed to notice a radiation-suited figure, flattened against the wall on the other side of the arch.

As the Doctor vanished through the door the figure snatched off its helmet. His face a picture of frustrated evil, the Master turned and hurried away.

After climbing endless flights of stairs the Doctor dashed into the attic laboratory.

He summed up the situation at a glance. 'Cut the power!'

'I can't,' shouted Ruth frantically. 'The controls won't budge!'

The Doctor studied the console. 'Reverse the polarity'.

'What?'

'Reverse the temporal polarity!'

Ruth snatched an inspection hatch from the top of the console, extracted a circuit, reversed it, and fitted it back into place.

Immediately the whine of the apparatus began dying down. In a few moments it had stopped altogether.

The Brigadier began moving towards the connecting door. 'Is it safe to go in there?'

Ruth shook her head. 'No, wait . . .'

'But what about that poor chap in there?'

Ruth held up her hand for silence, studying a rapidly falling dial. 'Right, the level should be safe now.'

The Doctor and the Brigadier hurried through into the inner lab. Kneeling by the unconscious body, the Doctor lifted the loosened helmet from its head.

The face beneath the helmet was lined and wrinkled, with the pouched and sagging skin of the very old. Above it was a shock of snow-white hair.

Ruth gave a gasp of horror. 'Stuart!'

The Doctor looked curiously at her. 'Who is this man?'

'Stuart Hyde – my assistant.'

'Your *assistant* – at his age?'

'Stuart's only twenty-five!'

'And this man's eighty or more.' The Doctor stared thoughtfully at the ancient face.

Jo Grant came hurrying in, released from her strange paralysis in the car. 'What's happening, Doctor? Were we too late?'

'On the contrary, Jo. I think we were just in time.'

It was some time later and Stuart Hyde was resting uneasily in his own little bedroom in the Institute's residential wing. The Doctor was taking his temperature watched by Ruth Ingram, Jo Grant and the Brigadier.

'How is he?' asked the Brigadier.

The Doctor studied the thermometer for a moment and handed it back to Ruth. 'We must get him to hospital soon, but for the moment he just needs rest. He must have been a pretty tough youngster.'

Ruth sighed, remembering Stuart as he used to be, with all the vitality and bounce of an exuberant puppy. 'He was.'

'Lucky for him. Otherwise the shock of the change would have finished him off.'

'He will be all right, won't he?' asked Jo.

The Doctor nodded. 'He'll survive.'

'Like that?' said Ruth unhappily. 'And for how long? He's an old man!'

As usual the Brigadier was still struggling to understand what was going on. 'But what caused it? Some sort of radioactivity?'

'No, it's more than that.'

'A change in the metabolism?' suggested Jo.

The Doctor rubbed his chin. 'That's more like it, but it still can't be the whole answer. Even if the metabolic rate had increased a hundredfold, the change in him would have taken seven or eight months, not seconds.'

The Brigadier gave up. 'Well, there's only one thing I know that makes people grow old.'

The Doctor raised an eyebrow. 'Yes?'

'Anno Domini, Doctor. The passing of time.'

'We all know that,' said Ruth impatiently.

But the Doctor said, 'Congratulations, Brigadier. You've provided the explanation.'

'Glad to be of service, Doctor. Er – what did I say?'

'Time,' said the Doctor impressively. 'That's the answer. The only possible answer. Stuart Hyde's own personal time was speeded up so enormously that his whole physiological life passed by in a moment. But why? How did it happen?'

Ruth shrugged. 'The Professor might know. But he seems to have disappeared.'

Jo looked puzzled. 'What Professor?'

'Professor Thascalos. TOMTIT's his baby.'

'*What*?' yelled the Doctor indignantly. 'The arrogance of that man is beyond belief!'

'Whose arrogance?' asked the Brigadier wearily. 'I do wish you wouldn't speak in riddles, Doctor.'

'A more classical education might have helped, Brigadier, "Thascalos" is a Greek word –'

'I get it,' interrupted Jo. 'I bet "Thascalos" is the Greek for "Master".'

Stuart moaned and stirred.

Ruth leaned over him. 'He's coming round.'

'Help . . .' muttered Stuart. 'Help me . . .'

'It's all right,' said Jo soothingly. 'You're safe now.'

The old man glared wildly at her. 'Safe? No-one's safe. He's here . . . he's here. *I saw him.*'

Ruth tried to settle him back on his pillows. 'The

37

poor boy's delirious,' she said. 'Don't try to speak, Stu. Just rest.'

'No, wait,' snapped the Doctor. 'Let him talk. What did you see?' He leaned over the terrified old man. 'Answer me!'

'Danger!' muttered Stuart. 'The crystal . . . *the crystal.*'

His body arched and he flung his head from side to side.

Ruth tried to push the Doctor aside. 'You must stop this!'

The Doctor ignored her, leaning over Stuart. 'Speak up, man! What was it you saw?'

'I say, steady on, Doctor,' said the Brigadier.

'Doctor, *please,*' pleaded Jo.

But the Doctor was not to be distracted. 'Be quiet all of you.' He leaned over Stuart. 'Stuart, answer me! *What was it?*'

Suddenly Stuart sat bolt upright. '*Kronos*!' he screamed hoarsely. 'It was Kronos!' He fell back unconscious.

'I should have known!' said the Doctor softly. 'Doctor Ingram, I want you to come with me. You must tell me everything you know about Professor Thascalos and about this machine of his.'

'Shall I come too?' asked Jo.

'No, you'd better stay here with this poor fellow. If he starts talking again, call me at once.' The Doctor headed for the door and with a helpless look at the others, Ruth followed him.

'Better lock the door behind us, Miss Grant,' advised the Brigadier.

The Doctor paused. 'Don't hang about, Brigadier, I've got a job for you too, you know!'

In the duty room at UNIT HQ Captain Yates was noting his superior's requirements on a message pad.

'Newton Institute, Wootton. Yes sir, got that, sir. Over.'

The Brigadier's voice crackled from the RT. Unfortunately, there was rather more crackle than message. Mike Yates flicked the switch. 'Say again, sir, I didn't quite get that. Over.'

The Brigadier was standing by his land rover which was still parked outside the Newton Institute. He raised his voice. 'I said, bring some men down with you, Captain Yates, I feel as naked as a baby in its bath. Light and heavy machine guns . . . oh, and shove a couple of anti-tank guns in the boot, will you?'

Mike's voice was puzzled. 'You've got tanks there, sir?'

'You never know,' said the Brigadier ominously. 'Over.' Although the Brigadier didn't really know what he was up against, he did know that the average alien menace seemed distressingly immune to rifle bullets. Maybe something heavier would do the trick.

Mike Yates said, 'Right, sir, I've got all that. And when, sir? I mean how soon?'

'Oh, the usual,' said the Brigadier calmly. 'About ten minutes ago! Oh, and Captain Yates, the Doctor wants you to bring his TARDIS with you. Over.'

'Right, sir. Over and out.'

'Over and out.'

The Brigadier turned as he heard voices behind him. Humphrey Cook and his assistant Proctor were marching out of the Institute, followed by a protesting Director.

'I'm sorry, Charles,' Cook was saying. 'The whole things smells of bad fish. You'll be well out of it.'

The Director seemed compelled to argue a hopeless case. 'But I would stake my reputation on the integrity of Professor Thascalos.'

'You already have, Charles. A foolish gamble at very long odds. It is scarcely surprising that you lost.'

'Humphrey, please . . .'

'I'm sorry, Charles. I see no alternative to a full Whitehall enquiry. One can only hope we shan't have to parade our dirty linen at Westminster.'

The Brigadier stepped forward. 'Forgive me, Mr Cook.'

'Doctor Cook, actually.'

'I beg your pardon, *Doctor* Cook. I couldn't help over-hearing what you were saying.'

'Well?'

'This affair is no longer in your hands, sir. It is now a security matter and I have taken over.'

'You have no right, Brigadier.'

'I'm sorry, sir, I have every right. Subsection three of the preamble to the seventh enabling act, sir. Paragraph twenty-four G, if I remember rightly.'

'Oh,' said Cook completely deflated.

'So, bearing in mind the Official Secrets Act, you will please say nothing to anyone about today's events.' He glared fiercely at Proctor. 'Either of you.'

Proctor opened his mouth to protest, but Humphrey Cook snapped. 'Oh, be quiet, Proctor.' He turned back to the Brigadier. 'You can't possibly have grounds for such high-handed –'

'This man Thascalos is known to me,' interrupted the Brigadier. 'He is a dangerous criminal and an escaped prisoner. Sufficient grounds, I think?'

Cook rounded on the defenceless Proctor. 'Oh, come along, Proctor. Don't stand about.'

They both got into the car, and Cook leaned out of the window to fire a parting shot at the Director. 'You will be hearing from me, Charles.'

The limousine swept away down the drive and disappeared from view.

The Brigadier watched it go with the satisfaction of one who has thoroughly routed the enemy. He turned back to the Director, who was walking back into the main building with slow, almost stumbling steps. 'Excuse me, sir!'

The Director didn't seem to hear him.

'Doctor Perceval!'

Slowly the Director turned, his expression vague, almost blank. The poor old boy was still reeling under the shock, thought the Brigadier. 'Are you feeling quite well, sir?'

'What? Yes, of course I am. This whole matter has been a great shock of course . . . What did you want?'

'I should like this place evacuated of all but essential personnel at once.'

'But that's nonsense,' spluttered Perceval. 'I can hardly think, Brigadier, that you have the remotest idea what you are asking. There are projects in train here which –'

'I'm sorry, sir, but it's absolutely necessary. Sergeant Benton is keeping an eye on that infernal machine of yours until the troops arrive, but I cannot be responsible for the consequences unless you do what I ask.'

The Director attempted a last protest. 'Brigadier, you may enjoy playing soldiers, but –'

The Brigadier said crisply, 'By three o'clock

please, Doctor Perceval.' He turned to go, then paused. 'By the way, if the Master should contact you, don't try to hold him. Just let me know at once.'

'Who?'

The Brigadier smiled wryly. 'I'm sorry. I meant the Professor of course. Professor Thascalos.'

The Director looked worried. 'But surely he'll be miles away by now?'

'I doubt it. Why should he have any idea that we're on to him? Believe me, he'll be back!'

5

The Legend

Sergeant Benton sat in the inner lab, staring unblinkingly at the TOMTIT machine. So far, no-one had tried to run away with it.

There was a tap on the outer door. 'Who is it?'

'Me! Ruth Ingram. The Doctor's with me.'

Benton got up went through the outer lab and opened the door, admitting Ruth Ingram and the Doctor, who looked quizzically at him. 'Any trouble?'

'I've been a bit lonely, that's all.'

'Good, good,' said the Doctor absently. He stared thoughtfully at the TOMTIT machine.

'But *why* won't you explain, Doctor?' asked Ruth, obviously continuing an unfinished conversation.

'Because I have to be sure that I'm right. Now, where's this crystal?'

'Through here.'

Ruth led the way to the inner lab and lifted off the transparent cover, revealing the crystal socketted into its place in the machine. 'There.'

The Doctor stared at the crystal in fascination. 'The Crystal of Kronos. Then I am right.'

Ruth frowned. 'Kronos? That's what Stuart said. *Please* explain, Doctor – that's if you really do know what it's all about.'

'You'll find some of it difficult to accept, I warn you.'

'Try me.'

'Well – luckily you're at least familiar with the idea of stepping outside space-time.'

'I've lived with the concept for months.'

The Doctor said solemnly, 'And I've lived with it for – for many long years. I've been there, and a strange place it is too.'

He paused staring thoughtfully into space – or perhaps into space-time. 'A place that is no place, where creatures live, creatures beyond your imagination. Chronivores – time-eaters – who can swallow a life as a boa constrictor can swallow a rabbit, fur and all.'

'And this Kronos is one of these creatures?'

'That's right. The most fearsome of the lot.'

When the Director finally reached his office, he found the Master sitting in the big armchair beside his desk, drinking his brandy and smoking one of his best cigars.

'You!' gasped the Director. 'What are you doing here?'

'Don't panic. Close the door and come here.'

'But they'll find you!'

'Not if you keep your head. Why should they look in here? Now calm down and tell me what's been happening – and don't fidget, please!'

Ruth Ingram said, 'But surely, Doctor, Kronos was just a Greek legend, wasn't he? He was the Titan who ate his children.'

'Exactly. And what's more, one of the children in the legend was Poseidon, the God of Atlantis.'

'Are you trying to tell me that the classical gods were real?'

'Well, yes and no. Extraordinary people the Atlanteans, you know, even more extraordinary than their cousins in Athens. If reality became unbearable, they would invent a legend to tame it.'

'Like the legend of Kronos?'

'Exactly! Kronos, a living creature, was drawn into time by the priests of Atlantis, using that crystal.'

'You mean that crystal is the original? The actual crystal from Atlantis?'

'It is. And your friend the Professor is trying to use the crystal exactly as it was used four thousand years ago – to capture the Chronivore.'

'And that's what you meant when you talked of the most terrible danger just now?'

'Do you mean danger to us?' asked Benton. 'Or to the world?'

The Doctor said gravely, 'The danger is not just to us, or our world, or even our galaxy, but to the entire created Universe.'

Puffing peacefully on his cigar, the Master listened to the Director's stammered tale of recent events.

'And now here you are,' moaned the Director. 'Suppose somebody should walk in here now and find me talking to you?'

The Master sighed. 'My word, you are a worrier, aren't you? Come here.'

Reluctantly the Director obeyed.

'Closer,' orderd the Master. 'Now, look into my eyes. There is nothing to worry about. Nothing. Just obey me and everything will be all right. Just . . . obey . . . me!'

'Obey,' said the Director dully. 'I must obey, and everything will be all right.'

'That's better. Now go and arrange for the evacuation like a good boy, and let me get on with my sums.'

The Master took pad and pencil from a table beside the armchair and began a series of complex and abstruse calculations. 'You know Director, it's some time since I found such a good subject for hypnosis as you've turned out to be. It's quite like old times . . .'

Calmed and reassured, the Director sat down at his desk and began a series of telephone calls.

The time sensor in his hand, the Doctor was examining the TOMTIT apparatus with the sceptical expression of a garage mechanic checking over a very old car.

'There are two things I don't understand. One is the unexplained power build-up you had. The other is the strength of the signal I picked up on my time sensor.'

'You said yourself,' Ruth pointed out, 'the time sensor picks up *all* time field disturbances.'

'Indeed it does.' The Doctor began wandering about the lab. 'But the signal was far too strong for a crude apparatus such as this.' Suddenly the Doctor stopped in front of a tall green computer cabinet, the needle on the sensor flickering wildly. 'Aha!'

Benton came over to him. 'What is it, Doctor?'

'I knew it had to be around here somewhere. This, Sergeant Benton, is the Master's TARDIS!'

'I'm sorry, but you *must* leave. At once, please,' said the Director and put down the phone.

He heard the Master muttering, ' . . . now, if E equals mc cubed . . .'

'Squared, surely?'

'What?' The Master looked up.

'E equals mc squared – not cubed.'

'Not in the extra-temporal physics of the time vortex,' said the Master irritably. 'Now you've made me lose my place. You're an interfering dolt, Perceval.'

'I'm sorry. What are you doing?'

'Trying to find the reason for that massive power build-up we experienced. It makes the experiment uncontrollable. Even the filter didn't prevent it.' The Master frowned. 'Logically, it just shouldn't happen.'

'Logically, it just shouldn't happen,' said the Doctor.

'But it did.' Ruth pointed out.

'It did indeed. So, logically there's only one thing to do. Wouldn't you agree, Sergeant?'

'Oh yes, sure, Doctor. Er – what, for instance?'

'Switch on the power and see for ourselves.'

Ruth Ingram drew in a deep breath. 'Right!'

She switched on the power.

The machine began its low whine.

The Doctor studied a dial. 'It's reading ten – already.'

'That's impossible,' gasped Ruth.

Benton was looking through the open door to the inner laboratory. 'Doctor! Doctor, the crystal's glowing!'

The Doctor came to join him. 'Sergeant Benton, you're a strong man. Go in there and pick up that crystal.'

'After what happened to that chap Stuart?'

47

'It's perfectly safe at this low level.'

'If you say so, Doctor.'

Sergeant Benton's faith in the Doctor was limitless. He went to the crystal and tried to lift it from its resting place.

It refused to budge.

'It's fastened down,' he grunted.

'It isn't, you know,' said the Doctor. 'you can see it isn't.'

Benton heaved until his muscles cracked. 'I can't shift it.'

'No, of course you can't – because it isn't really here at all. It made the jump through interstitial time. It must still be linked to the original crystal all those thousands of years ago.'

Ruth gave him a baffled look. 'Then where is this original crystal?'

'Where do you think? In Atlantis, of course.'

Lightning streaked across the night sky of Atlantis, followed by a great rumble of thunder. In the Temple, a neophyte shuddered with fear. The gods were abroad tonight. He was little more than a child, olive skinned and curly haired, a priest's servant and apprentice. He glanced at the glowing crystal on the sacred altar and braced himself to do his duty.

His bare feet pattering on the marble floors of the temple, he ran to where Krasis, the High Priest, stood watching the lightning flare across the night sky.

The terrified neophyte threw himself to the ground at Krasis's feet. 'Holiness! Holiness, come quickly. The Crystal is afire.'

Tall and gaunt, an impressive figure in his priestly

robes, Krasis strode across the temple to where the crystal rested upon the altar. It was glowing fiercely.

Krasis lifted his hands in a gesture of worship. 'At last, Kronos, at last! The time is come, and I await your call.'

From behind a pillar a tall young man stood watching, a look of fascinated interest on his darkly handsome face. His name was Hippias, one of the High Council of Atlantis. He had long been fascinated by anything to do with Kronos.

The phone in the TOMTIT lab rang, and Benton snatched it up. 'Sergeant Benton . . . Oh, hello, Miss Grant . . . Yes, he's here. I see . . . Yes, hang on . . .' He turned to the Doctor. 'It's Miss Grant. She says Stuart Hyde is coming round. He's in a bit of a state it seems.'

The Doctor was already heading for the door. 'Tell her I'm on my way, Sergeant. You'd better stay here on guard. Coming, Ruth . . . Doctor Ingram?'

'Ruth will do. Yes, of course I'm coming.'

They hurried from the room.

In the sick bay, Jo was still chatting to Sergeant Benton on the phone. 'Yes, I'm all right, honestly. No, not scared exactly, just a bit . . . well, you know, churned up. And a merry Michaelmas to you too . . .'

She heard a groan from the bed. 'Oh lor, I'm neglecting my patient!'

Putting down the phone, she hurried back to the bed, where Stuart Hyde was writhing uneasily. 'Kronos . . .' he muttered. 'Kronos!'

Jo leaned over him. 'Are you all right?'

49

Suddenly he opened his eyes and stared wildly at her. 'I felt him coming back!'

'Kronos!' He clutched her arm. 'Don't let him touch me. The fire ... I'm burning. I'm burning ...'

Jo pushed him gently back on the pillows. 'It's all right, you're safe now. It's all right, honestly it is.'

Stuart stared at her as if seeing her for the first time. 'Who are you?'

'Jo – Jo Grant.'

'Where am I?'

'You're in your own room.'

Stuart groaned. 'I've got the granddaddy of all hangovers.' He rubbed his forehead and suddenly caught sight of his hands – the wrinkled hands of a very old man. 'My hands. What's happened to my hands?'

'It's all right,' said Jo soothingly. 'It's difficult to explain.'

'Give me a mirror. *A mirror*. Where's my shaving mirror?'

'There isn't one,' said Jo desperately. 'I'll get you one later. Now, just lie down ...'

But Stuart had spotted his shaving mirror on the bed-side table. Before Jo could stop him he lunged for it, snatched it up – and gazed in the mirror at his own eighty-year old face.

'No ... no ...' he groaned. Tossing the mirror aside, he buried his face in his hands.

6

The Ambush

'Point zero zero three five seven,' said the Master thoughtfully. 'Good!'

The Director asked timidly, 'You've finished?'

'Yes, at last. So, it's back to the lab.'

'But they've got someone on guard.'

'Yes, I suppose they have. You don't happen to know who it is, do you?'

'A Sergeant Benton, I think.'

The Master smiled. 'I see. Well, I think I know how to deal with him.'

By now the Doctor and Ruth Ingram had arrived.

Stuart, a little calmer now, was trying to give some account of what had happened to him. 'It was just after the cup and saucer appeared . . . I was about to switch off when it . . . happened . . .' His voice broke and faded away.

'Go on, old chap,' said the Doctor encouragingly. 'You're doing fine.'

With an effort, Stuart continued. 'It was like a tongue of flame. Like all my body was on fire. All my life, my energy, was being sucked out of me.'

The Doctor leaned forward. 'Why did you say "Kronos"?'

'Because that's who it was.'

'But how did you know?' asked Ruth.

'I just knew, that's all.'

'You mean you heard a voice or something?'

'No, I just knew.'

'A race memory,' explained the Doctor. 'We all have them.'

'What *is* Kronos?' asked Jo. 'Or should I say who?'

'Later, Jo, later.' The Doctor turned back to Stuart. 'Go on, what else?'

'Nothing else . . . till I woke up like this.' There was anguish in Stuart's voice. 'Doc, am I really an old man now? Is there anything you can do – or am I stuck like this?'

The Doctor hesitated. 'I don't know. But I promise you – we'll do everything we can.'

The phone rang in the TOMTIT laboratory. Sergeant Benton snatched it up, hoping it would be news of his relief. 'Hullo?'

He heard the quavering tones of the Director. 'Is that Sergeant Benton?'

'Yes.'

'This is the Director. The Brigadier wants you to meet him at once – here, back at the main house.'

'But I don't get it. Back at the house?'

'At once.'

'But that means leaving the lab unguarded.'

'Ah . . . well, he said to be sure to lock up. Those were his very words.'

'I don't know, Doctor Perceval,' said Benton worriedly. 'You put me in a bit of a spot. The Brig told me to stay here, no matter what. He'll have my stripes if I don't.'

In the Director's study the Master hissed, 'What's the matter?'

The Director said, 'Hold the line a moment please, Sergeant,' and put his hand over the mouthpiece. 'I don't think he believes me.'

'I'm not surprised, I've seldom heard a more inept performance. Tell him to ring the Brigadier for confirmation.'

'But you can't –'

'Do as I tell you.'

The Director took his hand from the mouthpiece. 'Sergeant Benton? I suggest you check with the Brigadier personally.' He paused. 'Oh, you want his number?' The Director looked helplessly at the Master who pointed wearily to the other telephone on the desk. The Director swallowed. 'I think you can get him on five-three-four. Yes, that is correct. Goodbye.'

A minute later the other phone rang. To the Director's amazement the Master picked it up and spoke, not in his own voice but that of the Brigadier. 'Lethbridge-Stewart. That you, Benton?'

In the lab Benton said, 'Yes sir. I've just had rather a peculiar phone call.'

'Nothing peculiar about it, my dear fellow,' said the familiar voice. 'Perfectly simple. I need you over here at the gate house. On the double.'

'Yessir,' said Benton woodenly. 'I quite understand, sir. Right away.'

He put down the phone and stood considering for a moment. He went to the window and opened it wide from the bottom and left the laboratory by the main door, locking it behind him.

The Director stood staring anxiously out of his study window while the Master stood idly leafing through a sheaf of calculations.

Without looking up the Master said, 'Well?'

The Director shook his head. 'No sign of him. Do you really think he'll – Ah, just a moment. There he is!'

The tall figure of Sergeant Benton came through the arch and rounded the corner of the gate house. 'It worked! It really worked!'

'Of course it worked,' said the Master sharply. 'Now see if the corridor's clear.'

The Director went to the study door and peered out. 'Not a soul, Professor.'

Tucking his notebook in his pocket, the Master led the way from the room.

Sergeant Benton meanwhile was clambering across the roof of an outbuilding just beneath the laboratory. He climbed a fire escape ladder bolted to the wall, swung agilely across to a nearby drainpipe and climbed through the window that he himself had left open. Back in the lab he closed the window and stood just to one side of it, looking out.

A few minutes later he saw the Master and the Director come out of a side door and hurry across the courtyard towards him. Drawing his service revolver, Benton ducked out of sight behind the TOMTIT machine and waited.

Before long he heard a key turn in the lock – naturally, the Director would have keys, he thought – and the lab door opened. He heard voices. First the Director.

'But Professor, you haven't much time.'

Then the Master. 'Time? Soon I shall have all the time in the world – literally!'

'In an hour or so the place will be swarming with soldiers.'

'Perceval, you irritate me. Be quiet! I tell you, nothing and nobody can stop me now.'

Sergeant Benton couldn't help feeling that this was his cue. He rose slowly from behind his hiding place, revolver levelled. 'Put your hands in the air, both of you.' The two men obeyed. 'Now, turn round – slowly!'

The Master swung round, an expression of sheer astonishment on his face. 'Well, well, well. The resourceful Sergeant Benton.'

'You didn't really think you could fool me with a fake telephone call, did you? It's the oldest trick in the book.'

'I underestimated you, Sergeant. How did you know?'

'Simple. The Brigadier's not in the habit of calling Sergeants "my dear fellow".'

'Ah, the tribal taboos of Army etiquette,' sneered the Master. 'I find it difficult to identify with such primitive absurdities.'

Benton grinned with savage enjoyment. 'Primitive or not, mate, you're still in the soup without a ladle – aren't you?'

The Master came forward. 'You must let me explain . . .'

Benton raised the revolver. 'Keep back.'

The Master stopped his advance, hands raised. 'Of course, of course. You see, Sergeant, the whole point is . . .'

Suddenly his eyes widened as he looked over

Benton's shoulder. 'Doctor, what a very timely arrival!'

Benton's eyes only flickered for a fraction of a second, but it was enough.

The Master sprang forward with tigerish speed, wrenched the gun from his hand and threw him against the wall with such force that he slid stunned to the ground. The Master looked down at him. 'You were wrong, Sergeant Benton. *That* is the oldest trick in the book!'

Turning away, the Master hurried to the TOMTIT apparatus and switched it on.

'What are you doing?' quavered the Director.

'I am going to bring someone here who will help me to find the power I need. Without it I am helpless.'

'I don't understand . . .'

'Of course you don't understand. How could you understand? Only one thing stands between me and total power over the Earth – over the Universe itself. He who I am calling here will show me how to harness that power. Now – you watch that crystal!'

The whine of the apparatus rose to a sort of triumphant howl. The crystal glowed brighter and brighter, till the whole room was filled with its blazing light.

Sergeant Benton, slowly recovering consciousness, opened his eyes and found himself staring straight into the glowing heart of the crystal.

And there, in the centre of that radiance, a shape was beginning to form . . .

7

The High Priest

To Benton's unbelieving astonishment the shape grew larger, became solid and real.

Suddenly an extraordinary figure was standing beside the crystal – a tall gaunt old man, in flowing white robes, a short red cloak and a jewelled breastplate. His long grey hair was bound with a circlet of silver and his haggard, lined face was filled with power and authority. A gold medallion hung about his neck. He was Krasis, High Priest of Atlantis.

Since the crystal in the temple had begun to glow, Krasis had kept ceaseless vigil by the altar, purifying himself by prayer and fasting.

At last the summons had come. The fire of the crystal had reached out, enveloped him, and transported him to this strange place.

The Master strode into the inner lab and spread out his hands in greeting. 'Welcome! Welcome!'

The old man drew himself up proudly. 'I am Krasis, High Priest of the Temple of Poseidon in Atlantis.'

'Of *Poseidon*? Surely Kronos is your Lord?'

'You would dare to profane with your impious tongue the great secret, the mystery no man dare speak? Who are you?'

The Master's eloquence was more than a match

for that of the old priest. 'I am the Master, Lord of Time, and Ruler of Kronos.'

'You lie! No-one rules Kronos!'

'I shall – with your help,' said the Master arrogantly. 'Together we shall become Masters of the Universe.'

Astonished as he was by these strange events, Sergeant Benton wasn't too astonished to gather his strength and choose his moment. The Master, the Director and the strange new arrival were all in the inner lab. Scrambling to his feet, Benton ran for the main door.

The Director saw him go and called, 'Professor!'

The Master swung round, but Benton was already disappearing through the door. 'Oh, let him go, he can do us no harm now.'

The Master turned to Krasis. 'Come with me!'

He led him through to the main laboratory.

Krasis gazed about him in wonder. 'Is this the abode of Lord Kronos?'

'No. But with you to assist me, I shall bring him here.'

Krasis fixed him with a reproving glare. 'I exist only to do the will of Kronos – and he is not to be commanded.'

'Ah, but surely Kronos obeyed the Priest of Poseidon as a pet dog obeys his master?' His voice hardened. 'The truth now, Krasis!'

Reluctantly Krasis said, 'So it is written.'

'Then you must have the formula – the secret of how to control him.'

'It is lost,' said Krasis sadly. 'For five centuries it has been lost to Atlantis.'

'And was nothing handed down?'

'Nothing save the Great Crystal – and the seal of

the High Priest.' Detatching it from its chain, Krasis held out the gold medallion.

The Master took it and studied it eagerly. The flat golden disc was carved with elaborate symbols. The Master studied them eagerly. 'But that's it. From this seal I can learn the correct mathematical constants. Kronos is in my power at last!'

Stuart Hyde had been carefully loaded into a wheelchair, and Ruth Ingram, escorted by Jo Grant, the Doctor and the Brigadier, was wheeling him out of the front door of the Institute towards a waiting ambulance.

Understandably, Stuart wasn't in the best of moods.

'Rest, that's what you need,' said the Doctor rather more cheerfully than was really tactful. 'That's all you can do at the moment – rest until your body recovers from the shock.'

'A charming prospect I must say,' grumbled Stuart. 'You'd better find out about my old age pension, Ruth. After all, I'll be twenty-six in seven weeks' time.'

'Try not to be too bitter, Stu,' said Ruth gently.

Suddenly Sergeant Benton came pounding towards them. 'Doctor! The Master's in the lab!'

The Master was carefully transcribing the mathematical symbols carved into the great seal. The Director watch him in puzzlement. 'But how can Atlantean symbols mean anything to you?'

'Comparative ratios remain constant throughout time,' said the Master confidently. 'If you have nothing intelligent to say, Perceval, keep quiet!' He

59

punched a complicated set of co-ordinates into the TOMTIT console. 'And now – we switch on!'

He turned on the power, and the rising whine of the apparatus filled the room.

In the inner lab the crystal began to glow. Krasis raised his arms in worship.

Sergeant Benton meanwhile was concluding what he himself felt was an extremely unlikely story.

The Doctor frowned. 'Are you sure he said he was from Atlantis?'

'Yes,' said Benton simply. 'He just appeared, from nowhere.'

The Brigadier wasn't interested in apparitions. He was only interested in the Master. 'Right, what are we waiting for? On the double, Sergeant Benton – Doctor! Females stay under cover, all right, Miss Grant?'

The Brigadier dashed off towards the laboratory. Benton at his heels.

'Brigadier, wait!' shouted the Doctor.

'And wait for me!' called Ruth Ingram. 'Females under cover indeed!' She ran after Benton and the Brigadier.

Jo felt suddenly strange and shivery. She heard a strangled cry from behind her and turned. 'Doctor, look!'

Stuart Hyde was recovering his youth at amazing speed. Grey hair turned to brown, the skin became firm and youthful, the eyes clear and bright – and suddenly there was a puzzled-looking twenty-six year old Stuart sitting in the wheelchair.

The Doctor studied the phenomenom thoughtfully. 'A massive feedback of time . . . We're too late, Jo. Kronos is coming!'

In the laboratory the crystal was pulsating, blazing with light. The Master stared into the heart of the fiery glow, raising his arms in a gesture of welcome. 'Come, Kronos, come!'

Krasis, the High Priest, stared enraptured at the crystal. Doctor Perceval, the Director, looked on in horrified fascination.

In the heart of the crystal a shape was beginning to appear. Perceval peered into the fiery glow, trying to make it out. At first it seemed like a giant bird, then like a man, finally more like a man with wings, though the head was still birdlike . . . He heard the steady beat of mighty wings. The winged shape grew bigger and bigger emerging from the crystal until it was somehow *there* in the laboratory, a shape of blazing white light thrashing about in the confined space like some great eagle in a too small cage.

Krasis prostrated himself in worship, but the terrified Director screamed and turned to run. The noise and movement seemed to attract the winged creature's attention, and it swooped down on him like a great bird of prey. Fiery wings enfolded him, swallowed him up and Humphrey Perceval ceased to exist, his very being absorbed by Kronos, so that not an atom of him remained.

As the Director disappeared, Kronos resumed the terrifying swirl of activity. The fiery wings thrashed about frantically, sending whole shelves of equipment smashing to the ground.

The Master was beginning to fear that he had raised a monster he could not control. 'Kronos! Be at peace!' he roared. 'I am your friend.'

Krasis raised his head, gazing worshippingly at the restless fiery form. 'You will never control Kronos.

He is the ruler of time. He is the destroyer. We are doomed!'

'Rubbish!' said the Master. A sudden idea came to him and he snatched up the Great Seal of Atlantis and held it out before him. 'Kronos, hear me! I order you to be at peace and obey!'

Kronos recoiled, and the beating of the wings lessened in intensity.

The Master laughed. 'Well, well, well! So, the pet dog does obey his Master!' He advanced upon Kronos, driving the fiery being back into the inner lab and slamming the door. 'Now, stay in your kennel till I have need of you!'

The Doctor and Jo watched as the retreating figures of the Brigadier, Sergeant Benton and Ruth Ingram suddenly ceased to retreat and became motionless.

Still striving to move forward, their bodies were frozen, like running figures when the film is stopped.

'What's the matter with them?' asked Jo.

The Doctor said, 'You stay back.'

He began running towards Ruth Ingram, the nearest of the group. As he approached her he felt the resistance of the temporal distortion. Forcing his way through it, the Doctor grabbed Ruth's arm and yanked her back towards Jo. As he retreated, movement became easier. By the time they reached Jo, Ruth was back to normal. She blinked and looked around. 'What happened?'

'That's it,' said the Doctor. 'She's outside the limit of the effect now.'

He ran forward and repeated the rescue operation with Benton.

Ruth looked on in astonishment. 'What happened to me? What's going on?'

'Don't worry,' said Jo reassuringly. 'The Doctor will explain – I hope!'

While Kronos thrashed about the inner lab like an angry eagle, the Master was working busily at the TOMTIT controls.

'What are you doing?' asked Krasis.

'Reducing the interstitial flow rate. Now don't interrupt me, I must concentrate.'

'You do not have the power to control him,' screamed Krasis.

'I shall have, never fear. Just give me time!' He made a final adjustment. 'Now – I must put him back where he belongs!'

The hum of power rose higher and, as it did so, Kronos began to dwindle and fade.

The Doctor led the astonished Brigadier back to the others. Since the Brigadier's own subjective time had been slowed down, it seemed to him as if he had been running normally when the Doctor appeared from nowhere, and hustled him back to his starting point at impossible speed. Not unnaturally, the Brigadier was both astonished and indignant. 'Doctor! Will you kindly explain . . .'

'There's no time to explain now. Benton, take the wheelchair, everybody inside, quickly!'

The Brigadier was still spluttering. 'What? What?'

'Come along, man,' said the Doctor impatiently, and bustled everybody away.

Kronos seemed to be rushing away, becoming both fainter and smaller at the same time. Finally the winged shape seemed to disappear into the heart of the crystal.

The Master mopped his brow, and said sarcastically, 'It's safe to go in now, most noble High Priest. Thank you for your help.'

Krasis followed him into the inner lab. 'I am no slave that I should serve you, I serve only the gods.'

'You will serve me, Krasis, and like it!'

'You dare to mock the High Priest?'

The Master stretched out a hand to the controls. 'Take care, Krasis! I can always bring Kronos back!'

Instinctively Krasis recoiled. 'No! No, I beseech you . . . What is your will?'

'Knowledge!' said the Master simply. 'Your knowledge of the ancient mysteries.' His voice rose in anger. '*Why* could I not control him?'

Krasis said scornfully, 'For all your sorcery, you are as a child trying to control a wild elephant. A puny child!'

'But I have the crystal!'

'That crystal is but a part of the true Crystal of Kronos.'

The Master was furious. '*A part*!'

'Only a small fraction,' said Krasis loftily.

'A fraction – and the rest is in Atlantis?'

'Deep in the vaults of the Temple of Poseidon. Guarded night and day from such thieves as you. You may command the slave but never shall you control the Mighty One himself!'

The Master had already recovered from his setback, and his deep voice was filled with arrogant confidence. 'You think not? We shall see.'

He reached out and grasped the crystal.

8

The Secret

In the Great Temple of Atlantis, Hippias held high a blazing torch and pointed dramatically at the empty altar. He was a tall, exceptionally handsome young man with glossy black hair that fell to his shoulders in shining ringlets in the Atlantean style. Wearing only the brief Atlantean kilt, he was a noble and impressive figure. 'You see, most venerable King – the crystal is gone!'

Beside him, King Dalios was, at first sight, almost comically unimpressive. Just a little old man with long flowing white hair and a jutting beard, clutching his night-robe around him.

And yet there *was* something impressive about Dalios, the calm and wisdom that come only with great age. He looked thoughtfully at his excited young councillor. 'And Krasis?'

Hippias spoke in a deep thrilling voice. 'I was there, O King! The sky opened and a spear of fire was hurled by the hand of Zeus . . .'

'Yes, yes, yes,' said Dalios impatiently. 'I saw the thunderstorm myself. What next?'

'They disappeared,' said Hippias simply. 'Krasis and the Crystal together – like smoke! What does it mean, Lord Dalios? Are the gods angry? Has the time come at last?'

Dalios looked pityingly at him. 'You are young, Hippias, as young in years as in the Sacred Mysteries. What do you know of Kronos?'

Hippias gasped, at the sound of a name almost too holy to speak. As if reciting some lesson learned by heart, he said, 'The years of Kronos were the great years of Atlantis. Perhaps some day he will return to us.'

'That is my fear,' said Dalios solemnly. 'Our world is in great danger. Come.' He led the young man through a secret door, and down endless winding stairways, until they were deep in the heart of the catacombs beneath the Temple.

As they descended the final flight Dalios turned and glanced over his shoulder at the young councillor. 'How old would you think me, boy?'

'A great age, Lord Dalios,' said Hippias respectfully.

'*How* great?'

Hippias hesitated. 'Four score years – more perhaps . . .'

Dalios smiled a little sadly. 'A stripling of eighty summers . . . No, Hippias, when these eyes were clear like yours, I saw the building of the Temple. I was a witness to the enthronement of the image of the great god, Poseidon himself.'

'But that was – it must have been five hundred years ago.'

Dalios nodded. 'Five hundred and thirty-seven.'

Hippias gazed wonderingly at him. 'Lord Dalios, would you have me believe that you are of such an age?'

'I am,' said Dalios quietly, and led the way on down the stairway.

The stairs led to a short passage. At the end of it

there was a great bronze door set into a wall of solid rock. Dalios produced a massive key, and after a moment the door creaked open.

It was as if he had opened the door to a furnace. A fierce white light blazed forth from the doorway. Hippias staggered back, his hands over his eyes. 'What is the light?'

'It is the true Crystal of Kronos,' said Dalios solemnly. '*This* is the great secret, the veritable mystery. Now that Krasis has gone no-one but you shares that secret. You must guard it with your life!'

Hippias bowed his head. 'I shall, my Lord.'

Suddenly a shattering bellow came from the doorway.

Hippias looked at Dalios in alarm. 'Do not fear,' said the old man calmly. 'It is the Guardian.' He called through the doorway. 'Return to your rest. It is I, Dalios.'

The bellowing died away. 'Who was it?' whispered Hippias. 'You said that no other person shares the mystery.'

'The Guardian is a person no longer,' said Dalios sadly. 'A thing, a creature too horrible to imagine, half-man, half-beast. Come.'

Stuart Hyde's wing room was a sprawling untidy sort of place. A row of home-made shelves divided the living from the kitchen area and there were clothes, books and records everywhere.

Stuart, who now seemed fully recovered from his sudden rejuvenation, opened the door and gestured everyone inside. 'Make yourself comfortable – if you can!'

The Brigadier was still in a state of some indignation. 'All right. Doctor, what next? Having picked us up by the scruff of the neck and bundled us in here, what do you propose to do with us?'

'Nothing at all,' said the Doctor cheerfully. 'There's nothing to be done at the moment – except wait.'

Jo giggled. 'I seem to have heard that before.'

'Speaking personally,' the Doctor went on calmly, 'I'd love a nice cup of tea. How about it, Stuart?'

'I'll put the kettle on,' said Stuart amiably. 'Get the mugs out, will you, Ruth? How about a sandwich anyone? Only marmalade, I'm afraid.'

'I'd love one,' said Benton unwisely.

'This isn't a picnic,' exploded the Brigadier. 'One moment you're talking about the entire Universe blowing up and the next you're going on about tea. What's happening, Doctor?'

'A great deal, Brigadier. For instance, you were caught in a hiatus in time. Being without becoming, an ontological absurdity.'

'I don't understand a word you're saying!'

'It's true,' said Jo. 'I saw it. You and Benton and Doctor Ingram were stuck.'

'Nothing of the sort, Miss Grant.'

'Oh, you wouldn't be aware of it,' said the Doctor. 'Your time had slowed to a standstill too.'

'And all this is because of that TOMTIT gadget?' asked Benton.

'So it would seem. After all it did make a crack in time, didn't it?'

Jo blinked. 'A what?'

The Brigadier said wearily. 'Oh, a "gap between the now and the now", as Sergeant Benton would no doubt put it.'

Benton looked embarrassed.

The Doctor patted him on the back. 'Exactly, very

68

well put. So we're bound to experience all sorts of freak side-effects.'

'You mean, even leaving Kronos and the crystal right out of it?' said Ruth, coming out of the kitchen section. 'Marmalade sandwich?'

'Correct.' The Doctor began wandering round the room, collecting odds and ends.

She looked puzzled. 'But why weren't we affected ourselves, when we were working on the thing? *We* didn't get slowed down.'

'If you stand right under a fountain you don't necessarily get wet, do you?'

'I see,' said Ruth. She didn't, of course, but it seemed to be all the answer she was going to get.

'Well, I'm dashed if I do,' said the Brigadier. He noticed the Doctor's strange activity. 'Doctor, what are you doing?'

'Me?' said the Doctor blandly. 'Collecting!'

The Master completed the last of a long series of adjustments to the TOMTIT apparatus, switched on and stepped back.

In the inner lab the crystal began pulsing with light once more. With each pulsation the intensity of light seemed to fade a little.

The Master rubbed his hands. 'Right! Now we shall soon be ready to move.'

'But, Master,' said Krasis nervously. 'The Mighty One. He may return.'

The Master laughed. 'Fortunate Atlantis to be blessed with such a courageous High Priest. Never fear, Kronos will only return if I desire it.'

'But the crystal . . . what are you doing?'

'I am draining the time energy from the crystal. Otherwise we could scarcely take it with us.'

69

'We? Where are we going?'

The Master looked surprised. 'Where? Why, to Atlantis, of course!'

The Doctor was still gathering up his collection of odds and ends. By now he had accumulated a wire coat hanger, a set of keys, some kitchen weights and the top part of a broken coffee maker. As he continued his prowling round the room the Doctor muttered, 'He must be stopped!'

'Fair enough,' said the Brigadier hopefully. 'Why don't we get on with it?'

'Because without the TARDIS we can't even begin to find out what he's up to.' The Doctor peered round the room. 'I need a bottle.'

'How about this?' Stuart held up a milk bottle.

'No, no, one with a narrow neck. A wine bottle would do.'

'Moroccan Burgundy, for instance?' Stuart fished a bottle from underneath the bed.

'Yes, that'll do nicely. And the cork?'

Stuart scratched his head. 'You've got me there.'

Ruth came out of the kitchen. 'Will this do, Stu?'

Stuart grinned. 'Remarkable efficiency, the cork's still on the corkscrew. There you are, Doc.'

'Well done!'

The Doctor sat down at Stuart's battered table and began sorting through his strange assortment of objects.

The Brigadier was losing patience. 'Doctor, I must insist – what are you up to?'

'Delaying tactics, Brigadier! A small fly in the Master's methaphorical ointment.' With that the Doctor set to work.

70

As far as the Brigadier could make out, he was building some sort of a tower . . .

The glow of the crystal became fainter and fainter still, until at last it died away.

Krasis gave the Master a look of awe. 'The fire is dying. You are indeed the Master.'

Working in absorbed silence, the Doctor was happily fitting his strange assortment of oddments into a sort of ramshackle structure.

Jo and the others watched in fascination as he sliced the cork neatly in half, jammed one half back in the neck of the bottle, fixed a needle into the half-cork and fixed the other half of the cork on the other end of the needle thus creating a sort of pivot or axis. He took two forks and fixed them by the spikes into the upper cork so they projected like arms, one on each side.

Stuart leaned over to Ruth and whispered, 'Another nutcase!'

She nodded and whispered. 'Fruit-cake standard!'

Jo overheard them. 'You just wait and see,' she said loyally. But even Jo was beginning to wonder exactly what the Doctor was up to this time.

The crystal was completely inert now, and the Master switched off the apparatus. 'There, it is finished. You must help me to carry the crystal, Krasis.'

Krasis shrank back. 'No, no . . . I dare not.'

'There is nothing to fear,' said the Master impatiently. 'You will do as I tell you.'

Krasis gave him a look of sheer terror. 'Do not compel me, I beseech you.'

Somehow, heaven knows how, the Doctor succeeded in balancing the top of the coffee maker on top of the cork. With the two forks projecting like out-stretched arms, the whole thing resembled a kind of mobile, or one of those balancing toys which can be bought in novelty shops.

'But what is it meant to be?' asked the Brigadier irritably.

The Doctor laughed. 'You're a Philistine, Brigadier. It isn't meant to be anything it just *is*.' The rickety structure started toppling and the Doctor corrected its balance. 'I hope.'

'You mean it's just a ridiculous piece of modern art?' asked Ruth.

The Doctor looked hurt. 'No, no, my dear, it's a Time Flow Analogue.'

Stuart gave her a reproachful glance. 'Of course it is, Ruth. You ought to have seen that at a glance!'

The Doctor went on making adjustments to the nonsensical tower. 'The relationships between the different molecular bonds form a crystalline structure of ratios.'

The Brigadier sighed. 'Does that make any sort of sense, Doctor Ingram?'

'None whatsoever!'

'I thought as much,' the Brigadier said determinedly. 'Doctor, please stop this silly game at once!'

The Doctor was infuriatingly calm. 'Patience, Brigadier, patience!' He tapped one of the projecting forks and the whole contraption began revolving like some lunatic roundabout. It wobbled alarmingly, but by some miracle it didn't collapse. However, the Doctor clearly wasn't satisfied. 'Oh dear!'

'What's up?' asked Jo.

72

'It doesn't work!'

'You astound me,' said the Brigadier acidly.

'Bad luck, Doctor!' Stuart handed the Doctor a mug. 'Here, have a cuppa and drown your sorrows!'

'A cup of tea!' said the Doctor joyfully. 'Of course! Tea leaves!' Swigging down the tea in one long swallow, he began balancing the empty mug on the top of his tower.

The Master was still trying to calm Krasis's fears. 'I give you my solemn pledge, Krasis, the crystal is still totally inactive.'

Krasis stared fearfully at the inert crystal. 'It looks dead . . .'

'Of course it is, I promise you . . .'

Cautiously Krasis stretched out his hand towards the crystal.

'Right,' said the Doctor. 'Here we go!'

He tapped the projecting fork again. The whole contraption began to revolve. It spun faster, faster, faster, until suddenly it was glowing with a weird unearthly light . . .

The crystal was glowing too and Krasis snatched back his hand with a yell of fear. 'The crystal is afire. The Great One comes again!'

'The meddling fool!' snarled the Master, and rushed to the control console.

The Doctor's strange contraption was spinning faster and faster, glowing ever more brightly.

Jo stared at it as if hypnotised. 'But what does it do, Doctor? I mean, how does it affect the Master's plans?'

'It's just like jamming a radio signal, Jo. We used to make them at school to spoil each other's time experiments.'

Ruth stared at the strange contraption which continued to glow and revolve in defiance of all the laws of physics. 'I don't believe it. I just don't believe it.'

The Master adjusted controls in rapid succession, slammed home the power switch . . .

. . . and the Doctor's contraption exploded with a bang and a shower of sparks.

The Doctor stared philosophically at the smoking ruins. 'Ah well! It was fun while it lasted!'

A UNIT convoy was speeding through country lanes towards the Newton Institute. In the lead was a UNIT land rover, behind it a canvas-hooded army lorry filled with troops, and behind that an open truck, in the back of which was a blue police box.

The Master was carrying the crystal, still mounted in a section of TOMTIT equipment, towards the laboratory door. It was a considerable task and since Krasis was now too terrified to touch the crystal, he had to perform it alone.

Suddenly the static-distorted voice of Mike Yates crackled through the lab. 'This is Greyhound Three. Over.'

The Brigadier's voice came in reply. 'This is Greyhound, Greyhound Three. And where have you been, Captain Yates? Over.'

'Won't be long now, sir. We're about ten miles away. Over.'

'Well, get your skates on will you? We need the Doctor's TARDIS here double quick. Out.'

'Greyhound Three. Wilco. Out.'

The Master replaced the crystal and its TOMTIT mounting, and studied a watch-sized mini-screen strapped to his wrist. He had left the audio-scanner switched to the UNIT frequency and now the vision scanner had homed in on the signal. To Krasis's astonishment the little screen now showed the UNIT convoy going on its way.

He shook his head in wonderment. 'Images that move and speak, wagons with no oxen to draw them . . . this is indeed a time of wonders.'

'I will show you greater wonders than either,' said the Master savagely. Still studying the screen he began operating controls with his other hand.

Krasis looked on fearfully. 'Master . . . Lord . . . you are not bringing the Mighty One here once more?'

'Certainly not. Just a little demonstration of my power over time. Watch carefully.'

Mike Yates was at the wheel of the land rover, leading the little convoy. They were on a long straight stretch of road, completely empty.

Then, all at once, it wasn't empty any longer. A knight in full armour, lance levelled, was galloping straight towards them.

9

Time Attack

'Look out,' yelled Mike and swerved off the road to his right, jamming on the brakes. The two vehicles behind him swerved off to left and right in turn and the armoured knight clattered through the gap and galloped on down the road.

Mike jumped out of the land rover, now slewed off the road at an angle and snatched up his RT. 'Greyhound? This is Greyhound Three. We're stuck in the mud. Forced off the road by some goon in fancy dress, I think. Over.'

On the other end of the radio link, the Brigadier stared disbelievingly at his RT. 'Are you suffering from hallucinations, Captain Yates? Or have you been drinking? Over.'

'No sir, but I could do with one, I don't mind telling you,' said Mike Yates frankly. 'This character in armour just galloped straight at us. You know, sir, the King Arthur bit. And then he vanished.'

'In a puff of blue smoke, I suppose,' came the Brigadier's sarcastic voice. 'Really, Yates, you have been drinking!'

In the lab, the Master looked at the stranded convoy on his mini-screen and smiled evilly.

'And that, Captain Yates, was just a sample.'

76

He busied himself at the controls. Amongst its other functions, the TOMTIT apparatus recreated the powers of the legendary Timescoop of the Time Lords, forbidden by Rassilon in the Dark Time. The Master was enjoying this opportunity to try it out . . .

Captain Yates raised his voice and bellowed, 'Righto, lads, out of the lorry and get these vehicles out of the mud. Get a move on, I want to get out of here.'

There was a flat crack, and something spanged off the side of the land rover.

Mike Yates whirled round, and opened his eyes in astonishment. On a little hill not far away a handful of men had appeared from nowhere, grouped around a cannon. They wore old fashioned doublets and breastplates and round helmets, and they carried long muskets. Roundheads!

'Take cover!' yelled Yates – just in time, as a ragged volley of musket balls hummed overhead like angry bees. 'Hey, what do you think you're up to?' he yelled indignantly.

The cannon boomed and a cannon ball whistled overhead.

'Keep down,' shouted Yates. 'They mean it!'

Yates and his men peered from behind the flimsy shelter of their vehicles, and the Captain reached for his RT. Heaven knows what the Brigadier was going to make of this one . . .

'I'm listening, Captain Yates,' said the Brigadier impassively. 'Over.'

'Another hallucination, sir. Roundhead troops,

attacking us with ball ammunition. Cannon balls, in fact. Over.'

'Captain Yates, if this is some sort of joke –'

The Doctor interrupted him. 'Believe me Brigadier, this is no kind of a joke. This is deadly serious.'

'All right, Doctor, you tell me what's going on.'

'Don't you see? A horseman in armour – roundheads – the Master's using that crystal to bring them forward in time.'

'So why don't we get over there and stop him?'

'It would be suicide without the protection of the TARDIS.'

'Which is stuck in the mud being battered by roundheads,' said Sergeant Benton.

'We'd better go and fetch it then,' said the Doctor cheerfully. 'Come along, Jo. Coming, Brigadier?'

'Benton, you stay here,' ordered the Brigadier. 'If the Master pokes his nose out you know what to do.'

'Yessir.' Benton was determined that the Master wouldn't escape him a second time.

'Can I come?' asked Ruth.

'And me?' said Stuart hopefully. 'I've always fancied myself as a cavalier.'

The Brigadier shook his head. 'Sorry, you'd better stay here with the Sergeant. You're the only ones who can handle that infernal machine apart from the Doctor. I must ask you to place yourself under Sergeant Benton's command. Both of you, right?'

'Full of old world charm, isn't he?' said Ruth resignedly. She reached for her lukewarm cup of tea.

The Doctor and Jo were already sitting in Bessie when the Brigadier hurried out of the building. 'Do buck up, Lethbridge-Stewart,' urged the Doctor. 'Get in!'

The Brigadier headed for his land rover, a powerful new model of which he was very proud. 'Sorry, Doctor, matter of some urgency, better go under my own steam.' He got behind the wheel. 'Try not to be too far behind!'

The Brigadier started the engine and roared away.

The Doctor grinned wickedly at Jo and started the engine, and flicked the Superdrive switch.

The Brigadier wasn't yet fully aware of the Doctor's latest modifications to Bessie. He was considerably surprised when just as he was gathering speed on a straight stretch of road, Bessie flashed past him effortlessly and vanished into the distance . . .

The Master and Krasis were watching the battle on the Master's mini-screen.

It was still inconclusive. The roundheads' weapons took some time to reload, and their fire was far from accurate. The Master grimaced in frustration.

Krasis stared at him. 'But why? Why do you do all this? Do you fear this TARDIS so much?'

'I fear nothing,' snapped the Master. 'But I intend to go to Atlantis and I don't want my enemy to follow me.' He glared at the screen. 'Get on with it, you useless seventeenth-century poltroons!' Shaking his head, he reached for the controls.

So far Mike Yates had ordered his men to fire over their attackers' heads. But the roundhead muskets, although primitive, were still deadly, and when another of his men fell wounded, Mike Yates decided that enough was enough. He took a grenade from the arms locker in his land rover, sprinted forwards to a point of vantage, pulled the pin and hurled the grenade in the classic overarm throw, dropping to the ground as he did so. The grenade arced through the air and exploded . . . just after both roundheads and cannon disappeared.

Mike Yates raised his head and saw to his astonishment that his attackers had completely vanished . . .

The Master laughed. 'I could have told you that wouldn't work, Captain Yates.' He adjusted the controls yet again. 'Now, stand by to duck. Here comes the grand finale.'

The picture on the Master's mini-screen changed. Now it showed a tiny stubby-winged plane droning across the sky . . .

Ruth Ingram cocked her head at the strange putt-putting noise. 'What's that?'

Stuart shrugged. 'Sounds like a motor-bike.'

Sergeant Benton was peering out of the window. 'It seems to be coming from the sky . . .'

The Doctor and Jo were zooming towards the ambush site in Bessie.

'Something wrong with the engine, Doctor?' shouted Jo.

'Never! Why?'

'I can hear a funny noise.'

The Doctor made one of his astonishingly smooth stops. 'So can I. But it's not the engine.'

Jo listened. 'It's coming from over there . . .'

The Brigadier screeched to a halt beside them. 'What's up?'

'Listen!' ordered the Doctor.

The Brigadier listened to the strange putt-putting sound from overhead and looked unbelievingly at the Doctor. 'It can't be!'

'Oh yes it can,' said the Doctor. 'Displaced in time, but real enough. It's a V.1.'

'A what?' asked Jo.

'A buzz-bomb. A doodlebug. A kind of robot plane – a flying bomb! The Germans used them against England at the end of the Hitler war.'

'What did they do?'

'Blew up sizeable chunks of London,' said the Brigadier. 'If that engine sound cuts out, fall flat on your face. It means the bomb is on its way down!'

Jo pointed off into the distance. 'Look, there's the convoy!'

And there it was, just disappearing into a little wood that spanned the road some way ahead.

The Brigadier grabbed his RT. 'Greyhound Three, Greyhound Three, can you hear me Yates? Over.'

Yates's voice came back, badly distorted. 'Greyhound Three . . . only just . . . Over.'

'Yates, that thing is a flying bomb, and it's headed your way. Over!'

'Say . . . again . . .' crackled the voice. 'Must be . . . trees . . . cannot read you . . . Over.'

(The Master made a final adjustment and waited, smiling.)

The puttering of the engine stopped, leaving a sinister silence. The Doctor grabbed Jo's arm. 'Out of the car. Get down!'

The Brigadier was still yelling into the RT. 'Yates, it's a bomb! It's a bomb! Get out of it, Yates!'

To his relief he heard Mike Yates's voice coming

back over the air. 'All out, lads. It's a bomb. Dive for cover!'

There was an ear-splitting crash and a column of flame and smoke shot up from inside the wood.

As the echoes of the explosion died away, the Brigadier tried the RT again. 'Yates? Captain Yates? Can you hear me?'

There was no reply.

10

Take-Off

In Stuart's room Sergeant Benton was trying frantically to raise someone – anyone – on the RT. 'Brigadier, come in please. Greyhound Three, come in . . . Captain Yates, can *you* hear me, sir?'

Silence.

Benton gave the others a stunned look. 'It's no good, I can't raise them. They must have copped it.'

Inside the little wood there was a scene of devastation. The truck containing the Doctor's TARDIS had been blown clear off the road, and the TARDIS lay on its side in a little hollow. The other vehicles were slewed at an angle amongst the trees. Several of the trees had caught fire and there was smoke and flame everywhere.

A solitary farm labourer rumbled up on his tractor and stared at the chaotic scene in amazement. 'What happened then?'

A dazed UNIT sergeant was staggering to his feet. 'Dunno. Some sort of explosion.'

'I know, I heard it,' said the labourer simply. He pushed his cap to the back of his head. 'Funny that! It were just about here one of them doodlebugs come down. Back in 1944 that was . . .'

The Master flicked off his mini-screen. 'You know, I thoroughly enjoyed that.'

'You have destroyed this TARDIS?' asked Krasis in awe.

'Unfortunately it cannot be destroyed. But people can. We'll have no more trouble from them for a while.'

By the time the Doctor, Jo and the Brigadier arrived, UNIT discipline was asserting itself and things were sorting themselves out. The UNIT sergeant had taken command, and those who had escaped unhurt were caring for the wounded and checking the damage to the vehicles.

They found Mike Yates leaning against a scorched land rover. His face was blackened, his clothes were charred and he was bleeding from an ugly scalp-wound. 'Now you keep still, Mike, and take it easy,' said the Brigadier. 'You've finished work for the day.'

Mike managed a feeble grin. 'Sorry about the TARDIS, Doctor.'

'Don't worry, Mike. We'll soon have her on her feet again.'

Already a team of UNIT soldiers with ropes was busily hauling the TARDIS into an upright position.

The Doctor drew Jo aside, took the time sensor from Bessie and handed it to her. 'Now, Jo, I want you to keep a close eye on this. As soon as you see the slightest reaction, you let me know.'

'Right, Doctor.'

The UNIT soldiers had fixed their ropes to the labourer's tractor. At a signal from the sergeant, he began driving forwards. With the unwieldy dignity of a drunken dowager, the TARDIS was straightened into an upright position.

Much to his relief, Sergeant Benton had finally managed to raise the Brigadier on his RT. 'Very good, sir, I'll stand by. Glad you're all okay, sir. We really thought you'd copped it! Benton out.'

He put down the RT and turned to Ruth and Stuart, who appeared to be in the middle of a blazing row.

'It's a daft idea anyway,' Stuart was saying. 'I've had one basinful, I don't feel much like another. You heard what the Doctor said.'

'For a member of the so-called dominant sex, Stu, you're being remarkably feeble.'

Benton looked amusedly at their angry faces. 'Is this a private fight, or can anyone join in?'

Stuart turned to him as an ally. 'Boadicea here only wants to creep over to the lab and nobble the Master.'

'And supposing the time field is still working?'

'We shan't know that till we try, shall we?' said Ruth crisply.

To Stuart's horror, Benton headed for the door. 'Right then, what are we waiting for?'

'You're worse than she is!' moaned Stuart.

The Master's escape was still very fresh in Benton's mind. 'So you're suggesting we just sit here and let the Master treat us like a load of twits?'

'Look mate, you're paid to play James Bond games. I'm a scientist.'

'Oh, Stu!' said Ruth reproachfully.

He swung round on her. 'And don't *you* start! You'd be the first to clobber me if I mucked it up.'

85

'Well, you could at least have a go,' she said indignantly. 'Oh, why are men so spineless?'

'Look lovey, I'm not *men*. I'm Stuart Hyde, registered card-carrying fully paid-up coward!'

Benton and Ruth didn't answer. They just looked at him.

'Don't look at me like that! For Pete's sake!' Still no-one spoke. 'Oh, all right,' said Stuart wearily. 'I'll come.'

'Thanks, Stu,' said Benton solemnly. 'I knew you wouldn't let us down.'

Stuart grunted. 'Just give me time, that's all.' He grabbed a giant spanner from a shelf by the door and waved it martially. 'Well, come on then, what are we waiting for?'

The Master opened the front of the tall green computer cabinet like a door, heaved up the section of TOMTIT equipment in which the crystal was set, and led the way inside. 'Come, Krasis, we have work to do.'

Nervously Krasis followed.

He was astonished to find himself in a large and well-lit chamber – in the centre stood a complex many-sided shape. An altar perhaps, thought Krasis. He looked about him in awe. 'Master, what is this place? Is it a temple?'

The Master put down the equipment and the crystal on a specially prepared table next to the control console. 'Do not let it concern you, Krasis.'

'So vast a space inside so small a box,' said Krasis wonderingly.

The Master seized his opportunity to keep Krasis thoroughly overawed. 'My power is greater than your imagination can encompass. You just

emember that. Your only interest at the moment is
o realise that Atlantis awaits us.' His hands moved
ver the controls. 'First I must test the power levels.'
he console of the Master's TARDIS began throb-
ing with power. He studied the instruments and
odded in satisfaction. 'Good. A few more minutes
ecycling and we shall be ready to leave!'

By now the Doctor's TARDIS was standing upright
gain.

Jo came running up to the Doctor who was
tanding at the roadside supervising preparations to
et his TARDIS back on the road, and then onto
he now-repaired truck.

'Doctor, quickly! I'm getting a reading!'

He took the time sensor from her and studied it.
t's very low,' muttered the Doctor. 'And it's fading
gain. He must be testing before take-off, the power
rain would have been enormous . . .' He raised his
oice. 'Brigadier, the Master's on the move again.'

The Brigadier came hurrying up. 'Right, Sergeant,
et the Doctor's machine loaded up!'

'There's no time for that! I'll have to take-off from
own there.'

'I thought your TARDIS still wasn't working?'
aid Jo.

'It isn't, not properly. I intend to use the time
ensor as a homing device, and put my TARDIS
nside his. Then wherever he goes I'll go with him.'

The Doctor made his way down to the TARDIS
vith Jo and the Brigadier close behind him. He
aused by the TARDIS door. 'Well, goodbye, Leth-
ridge-Stewart. I'll make contact as soon as
ossible.'

'*We'll* make contact as soon as possible,' corrected Jo.

The Doctor raised his eyebrows. 'We, Jo?'

'We!'

'Nothing I can say will dissuade you?'

'No.'

'Oh! Well, you'd better come along then!'

The Doctor went inside the TARDIS and Jo followed.

Even when you knew the TARDIS was bigger on the inside than on the outside, thought Jo, the actual experience still continued to be something of a shock.

She looked around her. Something had altered something about the circular configuration of the walls. 'Doctor, the TARDIS looks different.'

'Oh, just a spot of re-decoration, that's all.' From time to time, the Doctor altered some detail of the TARDIS interior. More often than not he decided he didn't like what he'd done and reverted to the original. Dismissing the subject, the Doctor said seriously, 'Jo, you do realise that what I'm about to do is appallingly dangerous?'

'I've been in the TARDIS with you before.'

'Very well. You've been warned.'

Jo watched while the Doctor studied the still faintly registering time sensor, and made a number of minute adjustments to the controls.

The TARDIS console began humming gently, and the Doctor straightened up. 'The two TARDISes are now operating on the same frequency. Now for the tricky part . . . This is the time setting. It's critical to the billionth part of a nanosecond. Do you see?'

'No.'

The Doctor sighed. 'If it's infinitesimally low, we'll miss entirely and go whistling off to Heaven-knows-where. If it's too high, by even the tiniest fraction of a moment . . .'

The Doctor slapped his hands together. 'Whoomph! Time Ram! The atoms making up this TARDIS would occupy precisely the same space and time of those of the Master's TARDIS.'

'But that's impossible!'

'Of course it is. So, what do you think would happen?'

'Whoomph?'

'Exactly. Extinction. Utter annihilation. Still want to come?'

'It's my job, remember?'

'Glad to have you aboard, Miss Grant,' said the Doctor solemnly.

Jo gave him a mock salute. 'Glad to be aboard, Doctor!'

The Doctor grinned and operated the controls, and the TARDIS vanished with its usual wheezing, groaning sound. At the wheel of his tractor, the farm worker watched it dispassionately. 'Londoners!' he muttered disapprovingly.

Taking a circuitous route through the shrubbery, Benton, Stuart and Ruth worked their way round the building, and then dashed through the arch that led to the Master's lab . . .

In the TARDIS, the centre column of the control console was rising and falling steadily. 'Mmm, yes . . .' said the Doctor thoughtfully. 'Well, so far, so good!'

'How long will it take us to get there?' asked Jo.

The Doctor rubbed his chin. 'Well, that's the curious thing. No time at all, really. We're outside time. But, of course, it always seems to take a certain amount of time. Depends on the mood, I suppose.'

'What, your mood?'

'No, the TARDIS's.'

'You talk as if she was alive, Doctor!'

'Depends what you mean by alive, doesn't it? Take old Bessie, for instance . . .'

The centre column began slowing perceptibly, and the Doctor broke off. 'We're coming in to land already Jo.'

Suddenly a curiously familiar wheezing, groaning sound filled the air – and a large computer cabinet appeared on the other side of the control room.

The Doctor stared at it in dismay. 'Oh dear, oh dear! Well, it was always on the cards, I suppose.'

Suddenly Jo realised what had happened. 'The Master's TARDIS is inside ours, instead of the other way round!'

'Quite! Very curious effect, that. I don't quite understand how it happened.'

The Doctor switched on the scanner and found himself gazing into the swirling patterns of the time vortex. 'That's strange . . . Oh no, of course. We're seeing through the TOMTIT gap into the time vortex. Wait there, Jo.'

The Doctor strode determinedly through the TARDIS door.

After a moment Jo heard him exclaim, 'Good grief!' Then he called, 'Jo, come out here a moment will you?'

Jo followed him, and found herself standing in a control room like, and yet curiously unlike, the Doctor's own. She glanced over her shoulder – and

here was the square blue shape of the TARDIS she
aad just left. 'I don't get it!'

'Don't you? Follow me.'

The Doctor led the way across the strange control
oom and out of the door on the other side.

Jo found herself back in the more familiar control
oom of the Doctor's TARDIS – with the computer
:abinet that disguised the Master's TARDIS behind
ner.

'I still don't get it!'

'Oh really, Jo, it's quite simple. My TARDIS is
nside the Master's.'

'But his is inside yours!'

'Exactly! They're both inside each other. I should
aave expected that.'

'So what can we do now?'

The Doctor smiled. 'I'll give you three guesses.'

Jo pretended to consider. 'Wait?'

The Doctor snapped his fingers. 'Right first time.'

The Master and Krasis were back in the laboratory
and the Master was making a few final adjustments
o the main TOMTIT controls.

Krasis was looking out of the window. 'Master,
ook! Men in wagons!'

The Master hurried to the window. Coming up
he drive of the Institute was the UNIT convoy,
arriving at last. He hurried back to the controls. 'I'll
oon deal with *them* . . .'

The Brigadier was leading the convoy in his land
over. He came to a halt and the other vehicles drew
ip in line behind him.

The Brigadier leaped over the side of the land
over and began barking orders. 'Right, A squad

here, B squad round the back. Keep your eyes open. At the double no-oo-oo . . .'

Time suddenly slowed. To the Brigadier, every thing felt normal but, as the time field took effect Krasis and the Master saw the Brigadier and his men freeze like statues. 'That'll keep them nicely unoccupied for the time being. In you go, Krasis!'

Krasis recoiled. 'Where?'

The Master flung open the front of the computer cabinet. 'Into my TARDIS, man, and be quick about it!' Reluctantly Krasis obeyed.

The Master made a last adjustment to the TOMTIT console. 'They won't stop me now!'

The lab door was flung open and Ruth Ingram appeared. 'Sorry, Professor, that's where you're wrong!' Behind her was Stuart Hyde, nervously brandishing his enormous spanner.

The Master took a step forward. For all his moderate size he was enormously strong, and he knew full well that he could brush these two aside like cobwebs. 'Well, well, well, my devoted assist ants! And are you going to stop me?'

'Not by ourselves, no,' said Ruth steadily. 'Take a look behind you.'

The Master's lip curled in scorn. 'Oh, really! You don't expect me to believe . . .'

From behind him Benton's voice said, 'Suit your self mate. But you'd better get those hands up!'

The Master whirled round. Benton had just finished clambering through the window and was covering him with the big service revolver. Slowly the Master raised his hands. 'I should have finished you off when I had the chance.'

'You'll never get another one. Stuart, see if he's got a gun.'

Stuart moved to search the Master – and made the elementary mistake of coming between the Master and Benton's gun. It was only for a second, but for the Master it was long enough.

With one savage sweep of his arm, he sent Stuart spinning across the room. Then he dashed into his TARDIS, closing the door in Ruth's face as she tried to follow him. Seconds later, the computer cabinet disappeared before her astonished eyes.

In the Master's TARDIS, Krasis was pointing to a square blue shape by the far wall. 'Master, look! The other one. Your enemy is here!'

The Master gave an exultant laugh. 'Good! Now I've got him really trapped!'

11

The Time-Eater

Inside *his* TARDIS, the Doctor was being pitched about like a passenger in a small boat on a stormy sea. Jo was sent flying across the control room. She picked herself up and clung to the console. 'Doctor what's happening?'

'We're on our way, Jo. The Master's taken off for Atlantis!'

'But the TARDIS has never behaved like this before!'

The Doctor was struggling frantically with the controls. 'The two TARDISes are operating out of phase, that's why.'

Suddenly the TARDIS seemed to settle down a little. 'There,' gasped the Doctor. 'That's better. I've managed to calm her down. She has a very nasty temper when she's roused.'

'I never know if you're joking or not,' said Jo, rubbing an ache at the base of her spine. 'I think I've bruised my tailbone.'

'I'm sorry about your coccyx Jo, but these little things are sent to try us.'

'My what?'

'Your coccyx – your tailbone!'

Another voice said, 'I'm sorry about your coccyx too, Miss Grant.' The Master's face had appeared

in the scanner screen set into the TARDIS wall.
'How very sociable of you both to drop in!'

Ruth Ingram was staring at the still gently throbbing
TOMTIT apparatus. 'I think we ought to turn it off.'

Benton disagreed. 'I don't think we should touch
it.'

'Why ever not?'

'The Doctor was going after his TARDIS – and
that thing's some sort of time-machine, isn't it?'

'So?'

'So we'd better leave well alone, Miss.' Benton
couldn't help feeling that interfering with TOMTIT
might somehow foul things up for the Doctor.

'Very well. You're in command, Sergeant
Benton.'

'And a right muck-up I've made of it,' said Benton
bitterly.

'Come on, it's not exactly *your* fault.'

'Don't look at me,' said Stuart hurriedly. 'You
can't say I didn't warn you, now can you, Sergeant?'

'I'll listen to you next time. That was the nearest
I'll ever come to capturing the Master, that was.'

'Oh, come on, it isn't the end of the world after
all.'

'Isn't it? The Doctor seemed to think it might be.
No telling where the Master is by now – or *when* he
is for that matter!'

Ruth gave a sigh of exasperation. 'Honestly, you
two make me sick. Standing about moaning like a
couple of old women.'

Stuart was indignant. 'Old women?'

'Look, I mean it, Stu. Okay, so the Master's gone
off somewhere. And whether he's gone into the
future or the past – well, frankly I don't know and

I don't care. The point is, we're still here and now, and the first thing we've got to do is to define the problem.'

Stu had wandered over to the window during this little speech. At this point he turned and said, 'You can stop right there, Ruth, the problem is defined. Come and look.'

They joined him at the window and looked down at the Brigadier and his men, still frozen in their temporal stasis.

'It's the Brig,' said Benton wonderingly.

Ruth said, 'Exactly the same as before.'

'But how can it be the same as before,' said Stuart, 'now that the crystal's gone?'

'Don't you remember? The Doctor said TOMTIT works quite independently, even without the crystal.'

Benton looked alarmed. 'Do you realise this means we're trapped?'

'Now will you let me turn off the transmitter?'

They wrangled for a few minutes longer but at last Benton said 'All right, turn it off.'

'Ah, a man of decision!' Ruth hurried to the controls. The TOMTIT noise began to die away.

'Go on then,' said Benton. 'Turn it off!'

'I have.'

'But – they're still stuck!'

'That's impossible!'

Stuart turned from the window. 'Well, you'd better go and explain it to them, love. *They* still think they're stuck, apparently.'

'And we're still trapped,' said Benton. 'In here!'

'Now, Doctor, what can I do for you?' said the Master smoothly. 'Or is your visit purely social?'

96

'Oh, I thought we might have a little chat.'

'What an excellent idea. Why not join me out here?'

'Because one step outside my TARDIS and that would be the end of me!'

The Master looked hurt. 'You have a very low opinion of me!'

'You've noticed that, have you? Well, well, well!'

'It may interest you to know, Doctor, that I've put a time lock on your TARDIS. You cannot leave – unless I lift it, of course.'

'Do you think I haven't thought of that too? You're as trapped as I am. You can't even open your door unless I wish it.'

'Alternatively, I could fling you out into the time vortex,' the Master continued. 'I very much doubt if you could do that to me. So, do be very careful.'

'Do you really think I care what happens to me at the moment? Don't you realise that your plans could bring disaster to the entire Universe?'

The Master yawned and flicked a switch on his console. The Doctor's voice faded, leaving his silently mouthing face on the screen.

The Master turned to Krasis. 'An excellent brain, I must admit, if a little pedestrian. But what a bore the fellow is!'

'Is he dangerous?'

'Dangerous enough. But don't worry, I can deal with him.'

'In there?' asked Krasis. 'Surely, he is safe in there?'

The Master chuckled. 'As soon as he realises he's talking to himself, he'll be out in a flash.' He glanced at the scanner and saw the Doctor suddenly stop talking, his face indignant. 'Ah, he's realised at last.

That took a long time, the slow-witted fool. Now you watch. He cannot bear not to have the last word!'

The Doctor saw the Master wave mockingly and turn away from the screen. 'He's not even listening. He's turned down the sound!'

'Well, that's not very nice!'

'I've *got* to make him listen, Jo. It's our only chance of stopping him!'

'You're not thinking of going out there, are you?'

'Not if I can possibly help it!'

'What are you going to do then?'

'He's turned off his sound receiver, so I must make myself heard without it. "If the Thraskin puts his fingers in his ears it's polite to shout." Old Venusian proverb.' The Doctor reached into a storage locker beneath the console and pulled out a tangled mass of circuitry.

'Ah!' said Jo, wondering, as usual, what the Doctor was on about. 'What's a Thraskin?'

The Doctor was dismantling the assembled circuits. 'Archaic word,' he said absently, 'seldom used since the twenty-fifth dynasty. The modern equivalent is Plinge.'

'And what does Plinge mean?'

The Doctor was busily reassembling the circuits in a different sequence. 'Oh for heaven's sake, Jo, I just told you. It means Thraskin.'

Ruth Ingram meanwhile was carrying out a very similar operation on the inner circuitry of the TOMTIT machine.

'But why?' Benton was asking. 'I mean, when you

98

turned it off, the Brig and Co. should have speeded up again. Why didn't they?'

'Well, I'm not sure, but it looks as if TOMTIT has made a permanent gap in the structure of time. Our only hope is to close it up again.'

'And how are you going to do that?' asked Stuart.

'I'm turning the circuits upside down, so to speak. It's a bit empirical, but you never know.'

Benton looked baffled. 'Empirical?'

'That, Sergeant Benton, means I haven't a clue what I'm doing.'

'Join the club,' said Stuart cheerfully.

Benton scratched his head. 'So, it's just trial and error? Have a go and see what happens?'

'More or less!' She fitted the circuitry back into TOMTIT and switched on. 'Right, Stu, you monitor the interstitial activity. If it goes over sixty, give us a shout.'

'What's the upper limit?'

'If it goes over seventy, say a prayer and duck.'

'What do I do?' asked Benton.

'Just stay out of the way and look pretty. Right, Stu, are you happy?'

'Ecstatic.'

'Then let's have a stab at it.' She switched on, and the TOMTIT sound began.

'Interstitial activity, nil.' reported Stuart.

'Molecular structure, stable. Increasing power.'

Stuart began calling out readings. 'Three five. Four zero.'

'How's the time wedge?'

'Steady on zero zero four.'

'Right. Isolate matrix scanner.'

'Check! Four, five, five zero . . .'

'Interstitial activity?'

Stuart's voice was tense. 'Shooting up. Five five, six zero . . . It's running away again.' Ruth worked frantically at the controls. 'Decreasing power.'

Stuart's voice went on in a kind of chant. 'Seven five, seven zero, six five, six zero . . .'

Benton was leaning forward over the console trying to make sense of what was going on. Without realising it, he was resting one hand on the transmission platform.

'Five five, five zero, four five, four zero, three five, three zero . . .'

Benton felt a strange tingle running through him. He tried to snatch his hand away and found he couldn't move . . .

Suddenly he felt himself *dwindling* . . .

'Okay, that's enough,' said Ruth. She switched off and the power hum faded away. She hurried to the window and Stuart joined her.

The Brigadier and his men were still frozen in time. Despairingly Ruth said, 'It's made no difference. They're still stuck.'

Stuart turned back to the console. 'There we were the skin of a gnat's whisker from the big bang and —'

'Nothing happened at all,' concluded Ruth.

There was a strange wailing cry.

Stuart was staring in astonishment at the other side of the console. 'Nothing? Come and see!'

Ruth came over to look.

On the floor a baby was squalling indignantly as it tried to free itself from a tangle of army uniform. Benton, like Stuart before him, had been a victim of the TOMTIT's temporal interference, but in the opposite chronological direction.

Sergeant Benton was now just over one year old.

The Master waited patiently, eyes fixed on his monitor screen.

'Master, what is he doing?' asked Krasis.

'Exactly what I would do in his position.'

'And what is that?'

'Wait and see, Krasis, wait and see!'

Suddenly the screen lit up, showing the Doctor's face. The Doctor's voice rang loud and clear through the Master's control room. 'Testing, testing, testing! One, two, three, four, five!'

The Master laughed. 'I thought as much!'

'I've boosted my audio and over-ridden your sound circuits,' announced the Doctor, cheerfully. 'You can't turn me off now, can you? You've got to listen to me!'

'Have I, Doctor? Have I really?'

The Master's hands flicked over the controls.

The Doctor settled down to lecture the Master on the evil of his ways. 'Obviously you've not been able to bring Kronos through yet, or you wouldn't be going to Atlantis, so there may yet be time to make you realise your folly.' Suddenly the Doctor's words became twisted, garbled . . .

In his TARDIS, the Doctor listened in amazement to the sound of his own voice. What he had actually said was, 'Surely you must see the dangers you risk?' But somehow what came out was, 'Illursh ooee tsum ees uth serjnade eeoo ksirr?'

On the screen the Master leaned forward. 'I'm so sorry, Doctor. What was that again?'

The Doctor glared indignantly at him and shouted, 'I said, surely you must see the dangers you risk?'

But what he heard himself saying was, 'Eea dess, illursh ooee tsum ees uth serjnade eeoo ksirr . . .'

101

Angrily the Doctor switched off the scanner. 'Of all the low underhand tricks!'

'What happened? What language was that?'

'English,' said the Doctor indignantly. 'Backwards! He's picking up my words even before I say them, and feeding them back to me through the TARDISes' telepathic circuits, so that they come out backwards.'

Jo realised that the Master was reversing not the letters but the actual syllables of the Doctor's words. It was exactly like hearing a tape played backwards, but at normal speed.

'Did you say the TARDISes were *telepathic*?'

'Of course,' said the Doctor matter-of-factly. 'How else do you suppose they would communicate? Well, that settles it. I have no choice. Now listen, Jo, when I go out there –'

'You're not going out there!'

'What else can I do?'

'You said yourself it would be suicide to go out there without the protection of the TARDIS.'

'I've got to risk it, Jo. He's got to be stopped. But that's no reason to put you into any danger. As soon as I go through that door you must close it after me.'

'But then you'll be shut out.'

'And you'll be safely shut in. And you mustn't open up to anybody or anyone until I say.'

'I won't do it,' sobbed Jo. 'I won't.'

Gently the Doctor touched her cheek. 'You'll do as you're told, Jo. It's your job, remember?'

'But Doctor, if anything happens to you –'

'I know, Jo, I know. Now, go and open that door.'

The Master smiled triumphantly as the door of the

police box opened and the Doctor emerged. 'There, Krasis! What did I tell you?'

'Won't you introduce me?' said the Doctor.

The Master nodded to Krasis, who said proudly, 'I am Krasis, High Priest of the Temple of Poseidon.'

'Greetings to you, Krasis,' said the Doctor politely. 'Any friend of the Master's is an enemy of mine.'

'Oh come, Doctor,' said the Master wearily. 'Must we play games? I take it you have something to say to me before I destroy you?'

'Yes, I most certainly have!'

'The usual song of death and disaster? I do wish you'd learn a new tune, Doctor.'

The Doctor drew a deep breath. 'Now, just you listen to me for once. If you try to take control of the Universe through Kronos, you risk total destruction of the entire cosmos.'

'Of course!' said the Master arrogantly. 'All or nothing – literally! What a glorious alternative!'

'You're mad! Paranoid!

'Of course, Doctor,' said the Master. 'Who isn't? I'm just a little more honest than the rest, that's all. Goodbye, Doctor.'

The Master threw the switch on the TOMTIT machine.

The crystal began to glow.

'No, Master, no!' shrieked Krasis.

But it was too late. The winged form of Kronos was emerging from the fiery heart of the glowing crystal, and the beating of his mighty wings filled the Master's control room. Holding up the Seal of Atlantis for protection, the Master shouted, 'Behold, Kronos, a rare, a delicate feast for you. A Time Lord! Devour him! *Devour him*!'

Kronos swooped down, wrapped his fiery wings about the Doctor and engulfed him.

In the Doctor's TARDIS, Jo Grant had seen everything on the scanner. She gave an anguished cry of 'Doctor!' and fainted dead away.

12

Atlantis

When Kronos unfolded his wings the Doctor was gone, vanished leaving no trace behind.

His appetite unsated, Kronos bore down on the Master and Krasis, filling the air with the terrifying beating of his wings.

Krasis cowered away with a scream of terror, but the Master stood his ground, holding up the Great Seal of Atlantis. 'Kronos, be at peace – I command you! *Be at peace!*'

For a moment nothing happened. Then, with astonishing suddenness, Kronos began to shrink, to dwindle, and vanished into the heart of the glowing crystal.

The Master laughed exultantly. 'You see, Krasis? Kronos is my slave!'

Suddenly Jo's face appeared on the scanner. Her faint had lasted only a few moments, and she was desperate to discover the Doctor's fate.

The Master looked up. 'Miss Grant?'

'What's happened to the Doctor? You must help him!'

'Ah, he's beyond my help, my dear. He's beyond anybody's help!'

'That thing – that creature – really swallowed him up?'

'Now that's a nice point,' said the Master judicially. 'Yes – and no! Yes, it engulfed him, no it didn't actually eat him up. He's out there in the time vortex, and there he's going to stay.'

'Then he is alive?'

'Well, if you can call it that. Alive forever, in an eternity of nothingness.' The Master chuckled. 'To coin a phrase – a living death!'

'That's the most cruel, the most wicked thing I ever heard.'

'Thank you, my dear,' said the Master, modestly accepting what he saw as a compliment. 'Now, what about you, Miss Grant? You're an embarassment to me . . . as indeed is that antiquated piece of junk of the Doctor's.'

Jo was close to tears. 'I don't really care any more. Do what you like – just get it over with!'

'Your wish is my command,' said the Master courteously. His hands moved over the controls, and the picture of Jo on the scanner began to rock and spin as she, and the TARDIS, were hurled out into the time vortex.

The Master touched another control and the picture on the screen showed the TARDIS spinning away into the infinite nothingness of the vortex. 'Goodbye, Miss Grant!'

The sudden, whirling acceleration caused Jo to lose consciousness yet again. She awoke stretched out on the control room floor, with a strange sense of peace. The TARDIS seemed to be poised, at rest. Dozens of voices were whispering gently in her ear. *Jo . . . Jo . . . Jo . . .*

Somehow one voice seemed to dominate the rest. 'Doctor?' she said feebly.

Thank heavens you're alive, Jo!

'Doctor! It *is* you!' She sat up, looked round, and found she was still alone. 'Doctor – where are you?'

I'm nowhere, Jo. Still in the time vortex. The TARDIS is relaying my thoughts to you.

'What are all those other voices I can hear?'

Those are my subconscious thoughts. I shouldn't listen too hard if I were you – I'm not all that proud of some of them.

Resisting the temptation to eavesdrop on the Doctor's subconscious, Jo said, 'I still don't understand, you must be *somewhere*. Tell me how I can get you back.'

You can't Jo – but luckily the TARDIS can. That's why she's put us in touch.

'What do you – I mean, what does *she* want me to do?'

Go to control panel number three.

Jo obeyed. 'Okay. Now what?'

Lift the little lid marked 'Extreme Emergency'.

'Right.'

There's a red handle inside. Got it?

Jo lifted the lid and saw the handle beneath. 'Yes.'

Then pull it!

Jo grabbed the handle and tugged hard.

Nothing happened – until a voice behind her said quietly, 'Hello, Jo.'

She spun round and saw the Doctor sitting cross-legged on the floor, a little dishevelled, but very much alive. 'Doctor!' she cried joyfully and ran to hug him.

In the outer hall of the Great Temple of Poseidon, a royal council was about to begin.

The chamber was enormous, dominated at one

107

end by the huge statue of the god Poseidon. In front of the statue was a raised stone dais upon which were set two carved thrones.

The trumpeters at the great main doors raised their long curved horns and blew a fanfare. Immediately a richly-dressed procession of priests and nobles, the High Council of Atlantis, filed into the temple, taking their places before the dais.

Crito, the Elder of the Council, rapped on the marble floor with his staff of office. 'Open the doors!'

The doors to the inner temple opened and a smaller procession appeared. In the lead was King Dalios, his ornate robes contrasting with his unimpressive stature.

The woman who came behind him, borne in a litter by four giant Nubian slaves, more than made up for Dalios's unimpressive appearance. Tall and imposing, red-haired and voluptuously beautiful, gorgeously robed and with an elaborate jewelled head-dress, she looked every inch the queen that she was. This was Galleia, Queen of Atlantis, Consort of King Dalios.

Priests, slaves and temple guards flanked the royal couple as they took their places on the twin thrones. The assembled Councillors bowed their heads and once again Crito rapped on the marble floor with his staff. 'Peace, my brothers! His Holiness, the Most Venerable Priest of Poseidon, King of the Ten Kings will hear his Council.'

Before anyone else could move, the handsome figure of young Hippias stepped forward and bowed low. His voice rang clearly through the temple. 'Your Holiness, Most Venerable Priest of Poseidon . . .'

Nearly five hundred years of public life had made

108

King Dalios somewhat impatient of official ceremony. He leaned forward, cutting off the string of complimentary titles. 'Yes, yes, yes, I hear you, friend Hippias.'

Hippias bowed again. 'My Lord, may I speak plainly?'

'It would grieve me to think you would ever speak otherwise. Speak as a friend should speak.'

Hippias tossed back his long coiled ringlets in an orator's gesture. 'You are popular, Dalios, and the people love you. Will their love fill their bellies in the winter when the granaries are empty?'

There was a shocked silence. This was close to treason. Then Dalios spoke. 'Your words are plain indeed, Hippias. What would you have me do? Would you have me order the rain to fall?'

'Yes, Dalios, I would!'

'Have a care, Hippias.'

But Hippias was not to be deterred. His eloquent words rang like a trumpet-call through the temple. 'Indeed, I *shall* have a care. A care for the peace of Atlantis. A care that foolish superstition, old wives' tales, and the fear of old men shall not prevent our caring for them as our rank demands.'

Myseus, another young Councillor, stepped forward. 'He speaks the truth, Lord King. Many think as we do.'

'You know not what you ask,' said Dalios wearily.

'Must I be plainer still?' cried Hippias. 'I know quite well. I ask for the blessings our forefathers once enjoyed. I ask for the divine Power to be given back to the land from which it was so cruelly stolen!'

Now Hippias was adding blasphemy to treason, and the temple exploded in uproar.

Krasis re-appeared as the Master returned to the control room, looking sinisterly elegant in a black, high-collared coat.

'Master, why are we not yet in Atlantis?'

The Master was busy at the console. 'My dear Krasis, I must work out the landing co-ordinates as accurately as possible. Your people must realise immediately that I am the Master, that I come from the gods, and that I am bringing Kronos back to them.'

'Where in Atlantis will you arrive?'

The Master gave him a look of surprise. 'Why, smack in the middle of the temple of course!'

It took the intervention of King Dalios himself to quell the near-riot. He rose from the throne, stretching out his hands, his voice surprisingly deep and strong for such a frail old man, and called out, 'Brothers, peace, peace, I say. Be silent!'

And all at once there was silence.

Dalios spoke again. 'I shall speak plainly too. You ask for the blessings of the Golden Years. I tell you plainly, there came a time when Atlantis grew to hate them. What would you have, Hippias, if you were Master of Kronos, Ruler of Time?'

There was a shocked murmur. To speak the name of Kronos was near-blasphemy, even for the king.

'Would you have ten crops in one season?' Dalios went on. 'A surfeit of fishes, an ocean of wine? Then take the barren soil as well, the stinking piles of rotting meat, an idle, drunken, cruel people. I tell you plainly, the gifts of Kronos were a curse. That is why we, of our own choice, banished him and renounced them.'

'But Dalios —' protested Hippias.

Shocked, Crito intervened. 'Be silent, Hippias! The King speaks!'

Sulkily Hippias subsided and Dalios went on. 'I have seen a temple, twice the size of this in which we stand, fall through a crack into the fiery bedrock of the earth. I have seen a city drowned, a land laid waste by fire. So listen to an old man's fears. If Kronos should come again, I tell you plainly – Atlantis would be doomed. You hear me, Hippias? Doomed, destroyed, never to rise again!'

Hippias seemed about to reply, thought better of it and turned angrily away.

Dalios sat brooding on his throne for a moment. He knew, because he had seen it, that interference with the true course of time produced short term benefits and eventual disasters. The physical catastrophes were bad enough, the fires, the earthquakes, the floods. Far worse was the moral and spiritual corruption brought by too much ease and wealth. The gifts of Kronos had been given up just in time. They had come very near to destroying Atlantis.

Now Hippias was clamouring for their return. And he was not alone. There had been as many Atlanteans shouting in support of Hippias as against him – perhaps more.

The voice of Queen Galleia broke in on his thoughts. 'Listen – I heard strange music. There it is once more . . .'

An unearthly sound shattered the silence of the temple, and a strange shape appeared in the centre of the temple – a tall green box. It was, in fact, the computer cabinet from the TOMTIT laboratory; in his haste the Master had forgotten to reprogram his chameleon circuit.

The overawed Atlanteans drew back. Dalios raised his voice. 'Guards!'

Nervous but determined, the temple guards came forward, ringing the box with their three-pronged spears. The door opened and a black-bearded, black-clad man stepped out.

Finding a razor-sharp trident inches from his face, the Master brushed it casually aside.

Dalios stepped forward to confront him. 'Who are you?'

'I am the Master. I am an emissary from the gods.'

The newcomer's voice was deep and compelling and there was a murmur of awe from the crowd. Dalios however was not so easily impressed. 'Indeed? Any god in particular?'

The Master studied Dalios for a moment, realising that here was no primitive to be impressed with tricks and mystic talk. 'Of course . . . Why should you trust me?'

He snapped his fingers and Krasis appeared from the doorway behind him. Since everyone knew that Krasis had been snatched up by the gods on the night of the great storm, the crowd was more over-awed than ever. Even Dalios was shaken. 'Krasis!'

The Master said, 'Now do you believe me?'

'What do you want?' whispered Dalios.

'To speak of the ancient mysteries. The secrets of the mighty Kronos.'

There was a terrified gasp from the crowd.

'You are brave indeed, O Master,' said Dalios. 'An emissary of the gods.' He raised his voice. 'Brothers, should I listen to this man?'

Queen Galleia had been staring in fascination at the newcomer since his arrival. 'He has the very bearing of a god himself.'

'He appeared from the heavens, like Zeus,' muttered Myseus.

'I know of many such tricks,' said Dalios dismissively. 'Krasis?'

The eyes of the High Priest glittered fanatically. 'Most Venerable, I have seen – *him.*'

Dalios lowered his voice. 'You have seen Kronos?'

Krasis nodded eagerly.

'We must speak privately,' said Dalios. 'Crito, the Council is at an end. Come, Lady.'

Crito rapped on the floor with his staff. 'The Council is at an end. The King departs. Sound trumpets!'

The fanfare rang through the temple and the King and his entourage moved towards the inner door.

Galleia rose to follow and stood for a moment, eyes fixed on the Master. As he moved past her, he paused, his dark eyes burning into her own. He inclined his head, very slightly, not in the salute of a courtier to a queen, but as a greeting between equals.

The Master went on his way, and Galleia stood staring after him. 'The bearing of a god,' she said, almost to herself, and moved away.

But Hippias heard, and stood staring angrily after her. In his gaze there was all the bitterness of an established favourite who has been suddenly replaced.

The Doctor finished his calculations and looked up. 'There we are, Jo. On our way to Atlantis.'

'But I thought you couldn't just take the TARDIS where you wanted to. I mean you haven't managed to fix it yet, have you? Or have you?'

'Not entirely,' admitted the Doctor. I'm relying on the time sensor to lead us to the Master's TARDIS.'

'But not inside it?'

'I hope not, not this time. We'll soon find out!'

He operated the landing controls.

Krasis and Hippias, both awaiting the result of the Master's audience with the King, found themselves confronted by a second miracle, as a tall blue box appeared beside the Master's TARDIS. The Doctor and Jo stepped out. Jo looked round in astonishment at the massive temple, with its great statue, the robed priests and Councillors and the Greek-looking guards.

The Doctor beamed amiably at Krasis. 'Well, well, well, small world, isn't it?'

Krasis stared unbelievingly at him. 'You are still alive!'

'So it would seem.'

Krasis soon recovered from his astonishment. 'But not for long! Guards, slay them!'

13

The Guardian

Hippias stepped forward, raising his hand. 'No! I forbid it!' He turned to Krasis. 'Are you mad? Who are these strangers? Why should they be slain on sight?'

'They are the enemies of the Master – and therefore the enemies of our people and our land.'

The Doctor said, 'We have come to warn you –'

'Silence!' screamed Krasis. 'You will regret this interference, Lord Hippias!'

Hippias ignored him. 'Guards, take them to the King.'

In the King's simply furnished private chambers, Galleia stood quietly by the door, a silent witness to the interview between the Master and her husband. Her eyes never left the Master, who stood dominating the seated figure of the King.

But despite appearances, Dalios was proving difficult to impress. 'If the High Priest saw fit to break a sacred trust, is that good reason for the King to follow him?'

Once more, the Master's voice was deep and compelling. 'Krasis saw the crystal in my hand, saw Kronos himself, saw him dominated by me. Krasis knows that I am the Master of Kronos.'

'Krasis is but a slave at heart,' said Dalios dismissively.

The Master leaned forward, staring hard at the unimpressive little figure seated before him. 'Maybe But Krasis has learned that it is well to obey me.'

Dalios looked at him, with a mild, amused curiosity. 'You seek to make me fear you?'

The Master sat on the couch, close to Dalios staring deep into his eyes. 'Not at all,' he said, his voice deep and soothing. 'But if you will only see with Krasis, that I am the Master, then naturally you will obey me.' His voice deepened, became more urgent. 'You will obey me. *You will obey me!*'

To the Master's astonished fury, Dalios shook his head and laughed. 'A very elementary technique of fascination. I am too old a fish – too old in years and in the sacred mysteries – to be caught in such a net. You are no messenger from the gods.'

'But you saw me descend from the skies!' protested the Master.

Dalios chuckled. 'Tell me then, what of great Poseidon? What did he have for breakfast? Fish, I suppose! And what of Zeus and Hera? Tell me of the latest gossip from Olympus. Do tell me!'

It was a new experience for the Master to be mocked and not one he cared for, but he controlled his anger. 'I underestimated you, Dalios.'

'I am no child to play with such painted dolls Kronos is no god, no Titan. I know that, and so do you.'

The Master bowed his head. 'The King is old in wisdom.'

Once again Dalios laughed at him. 'Now you try to flatter me. You pull a string and wish to see me

116

dance.' Dalios's voice hardened. 'You shall not have the Great Crystal!'

The Master rose with as much dignity as he could muster. 'I shall go now, Dalios. I have nothing more to say to you.'

Even now Dalios had the last word. 'You have said nothing to me yet. When you find the true word to speak, I shall listen!'

Humiliated and dismissed, the Master left the chamber.

There was worse to come. Outside, he met the Doctor and Jo Grant, being escorted by Hippias to an audience with the King. Astounded the Master stared at them, literally speechless with fury.

'Can't think of a thing to say?' asked the Doctor. 'How very embarrassing!'

'How about, "Curses, foiled again"?' suggested Jo helpfully.

The Master turned and stalked away furiously.

'Come,' said Hippias, and led them into the royal chamber.

As they entered, Queen Galleia slipped away by the door that led to her own quarters. She had listened angrily to the debate between the Master and the King. It seemed wrong to her that the fascinating stranger had been sent away, unhappy and rejected.

It was a situation that could be remedied.

As Jo and the Doctor were shown in, King Dalios rose courteously to greet them. 'Strangers are uncommon in our land – though not this day, it seems. Who are you?'

The Doctor bowed. 'This, your Majesty, is Jo – Jo Grant.'

'Welcome, Jojogrant,' said the King solemnly.

117

'Surely, as in ancient times, a goddess has descended from Olympus!'

Jo was taken aback. 'But I'm not a goddess, honestly I'm not.'

Dalios chuckled. 'Of course you're not, my child. Forgive the clumsy gallantry of an old man. I fear I'm sadly out of practice. Hippias!'

'My Lord?'

'Take the Lady Jojogrant to the Queen while I talk with . . .'

'Oh, this is the Doctor,' said Jo hurriedly.

'With this learned man,' said Dalios.

'This way, Lady,' said Hippias.

Jo hesitated, looking worriedly at the Doctor. He smiled reassuringly. 'You'll be all right, Jo.'

Jo followed Hippias from the room.

Left alone, the Doctor and Dalios stood silent for a moment, summing each other up.

Dalios was a priest as well as a King, and, as he had demonstrated to the Master, an adept in ancient knowledge. He had the ability to see the essential nature of a man. Just as he had sensed evil in the Master, he saw the goodness of the Doctor and the honesty of his intentions.

'Forgive the roughness of your welcome,' said Dalios. 'Hippias has all the delicacy of a red-necked fisherman.'

'Nevertheless, he did save our lives.'

'Indeed,' said Dalios thoughtfully. 'He kept that to himself! Now Doctor, why have you come to Atlantis?'

In her private chamber, a room rich with tapestries and jewelled ornaments, Queen Galleia sat nibbling grapes while Lakis, her favourite slave girl, dressed

118

her hair. Lakis was an unobtrusively pretty brown-haired girl, quite eclipsed by the more flamboyant beauty of her mistress.

'Tell me,' asked Galleia, 'what did you think of this Master, Lakis?'

'He had the bearing of a god, Lady.'

'My very thought. In fact my very words. Are you mocking me, Lakis? Would you dare? No, I hardly think you would. Are you frightened, then? I shall not be angered by your reply if it is an honest one.'

'I like the Lord Hippias better,' whispered Lakis shyly.

Galleia tossed her head. 'A sweetmeat! A confection for a child's taste. This Master would not cloy on the tongue, as Hippias does!'

Lakis bowed her head. 'He is very handsome.'

Galleia stared into the distance. 'Handsome? Aye, he looked well enough, I suppose. But it was a face of *power*, Lakis. A man with such a face would dare to risk a world to win his desire.' She laughed. 'Hippias is but a petulant boy.'

'And a foolish one, no doubt, to trust a queen,' said Hippias from the doorway.

Galleia rose angrily. 'Foolish, certainly, to think himself man enough to love one.' She turned to Lakis who was fleeing from the room. 'No, Lakis, come back. The Lord Hippias is not staying.'

Hippias bowed. 'The Lord Hippias would not be here at all but that he has been sent on an errand by the King.'

'Then give me your message, boy – and go!'

Hippias turned and called, 'Lady!'

Jo Grant came into the room.

Hippias said curtly, 'Lady Galleia, may I present

to you the Lady Jojogrant. The King would have you treat her as an honoured guest.'

'How do you do?' said Jo. She held out her hand, then hurriedly withdrew it under Galleia's icy stare. With vague memories of old historical movies, Jo did a sort of improvised curtsey and said, 'Greetings!' This seemed to go down rather better.

Galleia inclined her head. 'Greetings Lady.' She looked at Jo's striped mini-dress and fluffy coat. 'You come from a far land?'

'Couldn't be much farther.'

'She fell from the skies,' said Hippias. 'Like the Master.'

'A day of wonders,' said Galleia.

'You can say that again.'

Galleia looked at her in surprise. 'Why should I wish to? Lakis, take the Lady – Jojogrant –'

'It's just Jo actually,' interrupted Jo.

'Your pardon. Take the Lady Jo to my maids and see that she is given attire more fitting for a lady of the court.'

'Yes, Lady,' said Lakis obediently.

'And hurry back, Lakis, I have an errand for you.'

'Yes, Lady.' Lakis led Jo from the room.

Hippias said mockingly. 'Are there no errands for me to run? A flower, perhaps, a token of undying love for some lordling of the Court? But no, it would be dead before it was delivered.'

'You are impertinent, Hippias. Remember, I am Galleia, Queen of Atlantis, daughter of Kings and wife to King Dalios. Have a care!'

Hippias bowed his head. 'Your pardon, I took you for another. I knew a Galleia once, you see, a woman not the Queen. A sweet and loving lady, I took you for her. Please, do forgive me.'

120

Galleia bit her lip in anger, then turned and sat down, her back to Hippias. 'You may leave me now.'

Hippias bowed. 'I thank you, Lady.'

He strode from the room just as Lakis reappeared.

Galleia summoned her. 'Lakis, come here at once. Come closer.'

'Lady?'

'Go to the Master. Go to him quietly when no-one is near and say to him one word.'

'What word, Lady?'

'Kronos.'

'Kronos!' said Dalios unhappily. 'Kronos . . . Kronos . . . Kronos . . . I am the last alive who *knows,* who remembers with a fear to twist the guts. And these fools would have me bring him back.'

The Doctor said, 'But why didn't you destroy the Crystal?'

'We tried,' said Dalios sadly. 'We merely split the smaller crystal from it. It cannot be destroyed.'

'Of course, just like the TARDIS,' muttered the Doctor. He looked up. 'The Great Crystal has its being outside time. Only its appearance is here.'

'You are a philosopher, friend Doctor.'

'If wisdom is to seek the truth, I am.'

'Then help me, Doctor,' pleaded Dalios. 'Help me to find a way to stop this evil man. Help me to save Atlantis from destruction.'

The Master marched arrogantly into the Queen's chamber and stared about him. 'Where is she?'

'If you will please wait, Lord,' begged Lakis.

He was already turning away. 'The Master waits

121

for no-one. I shall return when the Queen is ready to speak to me.'

Galleia appeared in the inner doorway. She looked at the Master with the sleepy, wide-eyed stare of the cat in her arms. 'Please stay,' she said calmly. She put down the cat, which strolled lazily from the room, and sat on the couch. 'Lakis, serve wine for this Lord – and then go. See to the needs of our other guest.'

With trembling hands, Lakis poured wine and hurried thankfully away.

The Master sat on the couch, close to the Queen, and gazed in her eyes. In his deep, mellow voice he said, 'You are beautiful, O Queen!'

Galleia purred, like one of her own cats.

Lakis reached the next room just as Jo appeared in her new court dress, a simple Grecian-style gown. With her hair redressed in Atlantean-style ringlets, Jo looked even more attractive, and certainly more sophisticated, than usual.

She surveyed herself in the mirror with approval. 'Wow, what a fantastic dress! Do you reckon it'll get mum's approval?'

Lakis stared at her. 'Mum? Do you mean Queen Galleia?'

'That's right. Let's go and give her a preview.'

Lakis held her back. 'No, I'm sorry. She does not wish to be disturbed, The Lord Master is with her. They speak of the sacred mysteries.'

'Kronos and all that?'

'It is forbidden –' began Lakis.

'But that *is* what they're on about?'

'Yes.'

'Right,' said Jo determinedly, and headed for the connecting door.

Again Lakis stopped her. 'No! You mustn't go in. You mustn't!'

'Listen,' said Jo reassuringly. 'I'll be as quiet as – do you have mice here?'

Lakis nodded.

'I'll be as quiet as an Atlantean mouse!'

Gently she opened the door, and stood listening to the low voices that came from the couch in the centre of the room.

The Master and Queen Galleia were rapidly coming to an understanding.

'You are a man who knows what he wants, Lord Master.'

'And takes it,' said the Master arrogantly.

'You want the Crystal.'

'And I am going to have it.'

'Not without my consent.' There was an edge to Galleia's voice.

The Master said smoothly. 'Of course not. Yet I am confident that you will give it.'

It would have been simple enough for the Master to hypnotise Queen Galleia. Already under his influence she would have shown none of the resistance of Dalios. But somehow it was more amusing, and more satisfying to his enormous vanity, to dominate her by the sheer power of his personality.

'Why should I help you?' asked Galleia.

'For the sake of Atlantis, Lady. Would you not see her restored to her former glory – rich, powerful, mighty amongst the nations of the world? Who would not wish to be ruler of such a mighty country?'

Galleia considered this alluring prospect – and

123

went straight to the point. 'No harm must come to Dalios.' In her way she loved the old man, though more as a father than a husband.

'Why should it? He will reign for many long years, the beloved ruler of a happy and prosperous people.'

'And you –'

The Master sighed theatrically. 'Purely because of Lord Dalios's great age, it might be well if he were relieved of the more onerous burdens of kingship. The reins of power should be in stronger hands – such as yours, Lady Queen.'

He placed a black gloved hand over Galleia's jewelled fingers. After a moment, she covered his hand with her other one. 'And yours?'

'It would be my pleasure to serve you . . . Of course, when the end comes for Lord Dalios, as it must come for all men, then perhaps . . .' Again the Master sighed.

The conquest of Galleia was complete. 'The Crystal shall be yours,' she breathed . . .

. . . but not so quietly that the listening Jo didn't hear. She strained her ears to catch the Master's next words. 'And where is the Great Crystal?'

'Deep in the earth, beneath the temple. Dalios has a key – and so has Krasis.'

'Then Krasis shall take me there!'

'I wish it were as simple as that. No-one can get near, save Dalios himself. It is certain death, even to try.'

'But what is the danger?'

'The Guardian!'

'Yes, but who is this Guardian?' asked the Doctor.

King Dalios sighed. 'A beast, a man, you may take your choice. Once he was my good friend, a

124

fellow Councillor. He was a great athlete, and just as I longed for the wisdom the years alone can bring, he craved great strength, the strength of the bull, and a long life in which to use it.'

'A harmless enough ambition, I would have thought!'

'And so should I,' said Dalios sadly. 'And Kronos granted his wish, as he granted mine. But in his sport, Kronos gave my friend not only the strength but the head of a bull. And so he has remained, these past five hundred years and more.'

The Doctor recognised the origin of an old legend. 'The Minotaur,' he whispered. 'I'm sorry, go on!'

'There is little more to tell. He determined that no-one else should suffer as he has suffered. Until the last day of his life, for which he longs so ardently, he will guard the Crystal. No-one can approach it. Even to try is certain death!'

'Well, Krasis,' said the Master mockingly. 'Would you like to volunteer?'

'No, Lord no!' sobbed Krasis. He had been summoned by the Queen for an urgent conference.

Queen Galleia said thoughtfully, 'Then perhaps we should send someone down who is skilled with the sword. One who longs with all his heart to seize the Crystal – and whose death would be of little account.'

'Who, Lady?' asked Krasis.

'One who will listen to you, Krasis. The Lord Hippias of course.'

Jo, who was still eavesdropping on the conversation, heard a horrified gasp from behind her and slipped back into the anteroom.

125

Lakis was frantic with fear. 'What can we do? What can we do?'

'Tell the Doctor, that's what. Take me to the King!'

'I dare not, Lady Jo.'

'Would you rather let this Hippias face the creature?'

Lakis shook her head. 'Quickly then.'

They slipped away.

Lakis led Jo down endless corridors until they came to the entrance to the King's quarters. A trident-bearing guard barred their way. 'Halt!'

'Take us to the King,' demanded Jo.

Crito, the Chief Councillor, stepped from the shadows 'The King is not to be disturbed.'

'But it's a matter of life and death,' protested Jo.

Crito smiled. 'It could be indeed – yours!'

Jo was about to argue further, when Lakis pulled her aside.

'Be careful – the Lord Crito is no friend to Hippias.'

'Oh, for Pete's sake,' said Jo impatiently. These palace politics were a great nuisance, she thought. Suddenly Lakis pulled her deeper into the shadows.

Hippias and Krasis were coming along the corridor, deep in conversation. Hippias was carrying a sword.

'They must be going for the Crystal,' whispered Jo. 'I'll follow them. You try to get in to tell the Doctor and the King what's happening.' Gathering up her long skirts, Jo hurried away.

She followed the two men along the gloomy torch-lit corridors of the palace, and across to the adjoining temple. She followed them through the secret door

126

behind the altar of Poseidon, and through the maze of tunnels below the temple. The winding steps and tunnels led lower, lower, until the two men rounded a bend and disappeared from view.

Jo hurried on, rounded the bend herself, and found herself at the top of a steep flight of steps. At the bottom she saw Hippias, sword in hand, stepping through a door set into the rock wall. She heard an angry bellow.

'No, Hippias!' called Jo. She rushed down the steps to call him back. But as she reached the bottom, Krasis appeared from the shadows and thrust her through the still-open door, slamming it closed behind her.

She found herself in a great stone cavern, dimly lit by a flickering torch set into a wall bracket, its roof supported by many huge pillars. Hippias was nowhere in sight, although his abandoned sword lay close to the door. She turned back and hammered on the door.

'Let me out,' she screamed. 'Let me out!'

A shattering roar came from behind her.

Jo turned and saw a terrifying creature stalking towards her out of the shadows. The body was that of a huge, immensely muscular man, wearing a leather loin-cloth.

The head was that of a bull.

The creature threw back its head, gave a savage roar, and charged towards her.

14

The Captives

Lakis was by nature a timid girl, but in this emergency she found unexpected reserves of courage. Waiting for a moment when Crito was talking to the guards, she dodged around them and dashed into the royal chamber.

Dalios was still talking to the tall white-haired stranger. The two men looked up surprised as she skidded to a halt. 'Lord King, forgive me! Lord Hippias and the High Priest have gone to the lair of the Guardian, followed by the Lady Jo.'

The Doctor leaped to his feet. 'What? Lord King, tell me how to reach them!'

The many pillars supporting the chamber roof were what saved Jo's life. The Minotaur moved quickly, but it was relatively clumsy, and the smaller Jo was much more agile.

Time after time, the creature charged with a savage roar. Time after time it was left baffled, swinging its great head to and fro as Jo ducked into hiding behind a pillar.

Unfortunately the space before the door was clear. Even if the door hadn't been locked, there was no chance of reaching it without being seen.

Jo flattened herself behind a pillar, gasping for

breath. She was getting very tired. The Minotaur however, seemed as fresh as ever. And if Jo once started to slow down . . .

It was searching behind the pillars now, looking for her. As the snuffling of its breath came closer, Jo prepared for another spring – and wondered how many more she could manage . . .

The Doctor came haring into the temple – and found his way barred by Krasis and a temple guard.

'Seize this intruder,' screamed Krasis.

The guard raised his trident-spear, but the Doctor was in no mood for interruptions.

Wrenching the spear from the guard's grip he swung it round horizontally and thrust it forward under the chins of both Krasis and the guard, so that they were held back against the wall on tiptoe. Maintaining his grip with one hand, the Doctor snatched the key from Krasis's belt with the other.

'Sorry to hold you up like this, Krasis, but I need that key!'

Snapping the trident across his knee the Doctor disappeared through the secret door, leaving Krasis and the guard gasping for breath behind him.

Somehow Jo had been driven away from the main door, into a network of tunnels and passages on the far side of the hall. All the time she could hear the bellowing of the Minotaur as it pounded after her. The creature was hunting her, she realised, driving her towards the heart of its maze.

The Doctor came through the door and looked around the underground hall.

'Jo!' he called. 'Jo, where are you?'

From the far side of the hall he heard a faint cry of, 'Doctor!' It was followed by a distant bellow.

The Doctor began running towards the sound.

The Minotaur's plan had succeeded at last.

Jo was trapped in a blind alley at the end of which was a shining mirror set into the wall. The Minotaur lowered its head and bellowed, ready to charge.

Exhausted, Jo awaited her fate.

Suddenly Hippias appeared behind the Minotaur. He had been lost in the maze all this time, tracking Jo and the Minotaur by the sound of the creature's bellowing.

Faced by the terrifying sight of the Minotaur when he had first come through the door, Hippias's nerve had broken. Throwing down his sword, he had fled into the darkness of the maze.

Now, seeing Jo in danger, his courage returned. 'Stay back!' he shouted. The creature whirled round. Snatching a blazing torch from its bracket on the wall, Hippias hurled it at the creature's head – and missed.

The crushing force of the Minotaur's charge sent him to the ground. Scrambling to his feet, Hippias dodged behind the monster, leaping upon its back in a vain attempt to throttle it . . .

Reaching up and seizing him in its great hands, the Minotaur held Hippias high above its head. It stalked towards the cowering Jo at the end of the cul-de-sac and hurled the struggling body of Hippias at her. Jo leaped aside. Hippias crashed into the mirror, shattering it into fragments and exposing the wall beyond. He fell to the ground and lay still.

Swinging round on Jo, the Minotaur prepared to

charge again – when there came another distraction. This time it was a shout of 'Toro! Ah, Toro!'

It was the Doctor. He had slipped off his cloak and now he was holding it so the red silk lining faced the Minotaur, and he was giving the traditional cry of the Spanish bullfighter: 'Toro! Hey, Toro!'

The Minotaur charged. The Doctor flicked the cape aside and the Minotaur shot past, missing him by inches.

As quick as any fighting bull in the arena, the Minotaur spun round and charged again. Once again the Doctor flicked the cape, and this time as the creature charged past he dealt it a savage chopping blow with his fist on the back of its bull-neck. The Minotaur stumbled and fell to its knees. It shook its head and bellowed dismally.

The Doctor turned and ran to Jo, who was watching terrified, pressed against a stone wall. 'Are you all right, Jo?'

'Just about! Are you all –' Jo broke off to shout a warning: 'Look out, Doctor!'

The Minotaur had lumbered to its feet and was charging straight towards him. The Doctor leaped aside, taking Jo with him.

The Minotaur slammed into the stone wall with such incredible force that it smashed a hole in the wall's centre section, bringing down not only the wall but part of the ceiling as well. There was a rumble of falling stone and the monster vanished beneath a pile of shattered masonry.

Jo turned and saw the shattered body of Hippias. 'He saved my life, Doctor.'

The Doctor made a quick examination. 'I'm afraid he's dead, Jo.'

The Doctor saw a gleam of light beyond the shattered wall and peered into the chamber beyond. 'It's the Crystal Jo. The Crystal of Kronos!'

They clambered through the gap, and seconds later they were standing before a circular stone altar on top of which reposed a huge glowing crystal, a larger version of the one used in the TOMTIT machine.

The Doctor pointed. 'There you are, Jo, that's what all the fuss is about.'

'It's beautiful – but at the same time it's horrible. It gives me a funny feeling.'

'Cheer up, Jo. Now we've got the Crystal, the Master's little game is at an end.

'Not quite,' said a voice behind them.

They turned and saw Krasis and several temple guards. They must have reached the chamber by its proper entrance, thought the Doctor.

'The game is just beginning,' said Krasis triumphantly. 'A pity that you will not live to see the end.'

'That's where you're mistaken, Krasis,' said the Doctor firmly. 'And if you value your own life you will take me to see the King!'

The Doctor stared indignantly at the black clad-figure in Dalios's chair. 'I asked to see the King!'

The Master smiled and spread his hands. 'But I *am* the King, Doctor – for all practical purposes. Didn't Krasis tell you? A jolly fellow, our Krasis. He loves a joke!'

The Doctor glared at Krasis's malignant face. 'Does he really?'

The Master settled himself comfortably in Dalios's chair. 'A complete success, our little palace revolution.'

'What's happened to King Dalios?'

'Why, nothing, Doctor.'

Queen Galleia entered. The Master rose and bowed.

The Doctor gave her a quick glance. 'So Dalios is still alive?'

'Of course,' said the Master. 'Alive and treated honourably.'

Galleia came majestically towards them. 'Even though Dalios is an old man, the King is still the King.'

The Master gestured towards the Doctor and Jo. 'And now it seems I must thank you both!'

'What for?' asked Jo.

'Why for giving me the Great Crystal, Miss Grant.'

The Doctor glared indignantly at him. 'You don't mean to say you still intend to go ahead with this stupid plan?'

'I most certainly do, Doctor. And tomorrow, you will both receive a suitable reward – an introduction to the mighty Kronos. This time there will be no mistakes!'

'I wouldn't count on that,' said the Doctor angrily.

The Master snapped his fingers. 'Take them away!'

The Doctor and Jo were led away.

The Master turned to Galleia. 'You seem discontented, my love. You would question my decision?'

'Perhaps. It depends what you mean to do.'

'You must learn to obey, my love. To do my will. To carry out my commands like a soldier.'

Galleia's eyes blazed angrily. 'Or like a servant girl? You must learn, *my love,* that Galleia is a Queen.' She strode disdainfully away.

133

The Master stroked his beard and sighed. It looked as if their association was to be a short-lived one after all.

The Doctor and Jo were both chained to the wall in the same bare stone cell. They were reacting to imprisonment very differently.

The Doctor was leaning against the wall in the most comfortable position he could manage – which wasn't very comfortable at all. Jo, meanwhile, was wrestling frantically with her chains.

'Any luck?' asked the Doctor.

She shook her head. 'They didn't include Atlantean chains in my UNIT escapology lessons. It's no good.'

The Doctor nodded consolingly. He had given their chains a thorough inspection on their arrival, and decided that, since he had left his sonic screwdriver in the laboratory, there was nothing to be done.

Moreover, he was in a strangely philosophical mood, as if he had only to bide his time and somehow things would work out. A strange feeling for someone chained to a dungeon wall and condemned to annihilation . . .

Jo felt no such optimism. 'Doctor, what are we going to do?'

'We'll just have to play it by ear.'

'What will happen if the Master wins?'

'The whole of creation is very delicately balanced in cosmic terms, Jo,' said the Doctor thoughtfully. 'If the Master opens the floodgates of Kronos's power, all order and all structure will be swept away and nothing will be left but chaos.'

'It makes everything seem so – pointless.'

The Doctor smiled at her. 'I felt like that once, when I was young. It was the blackest day of my life.'

Jo looked curiously at him. It was very seldom that the Doctor embarked upon any kind of personal reminiscence. 'Why was that?'

'Ah well, that's another story. I'll tell you about it one day. The point is, that day was not only my blackest, it was also my best.'

'What do you mean?'

His eyes gazing into the past, the Doctor began to speak. 'When I was a little boy we used to live in a house that was perched halfway up the top of a mountain. Above our house near the mountain peak, there sat under a tree an old man. A hermit, a monk . . . He'd lived under this tree for half his lifetime, so they said, and had learnt the secret of life. So, when my black day came, I went and asked him to help me.'

'And he told you the secret?'

The Doctor nodded.

'Well, what was it?'

'I'm coming to that, Jo, in my own time. I'll never forget what it was like up there . . . All bleak and cold, just a few bare rocks with some weeds sprouting from them and some pathetic little patches of sludgy snow. It was just grey. Grey, grey, grey . . . The tree the old man sat under was ancient and twisted, and the old man himself – he was as brittle and as dry as a leaf in the Autumn.'

'But what did he *say*?'

'Nothing,' said the Doctor simply. 'Not a word. He just sat there, expressionless, while I poured out my troubles. I was too unhappy even for tears, I remember. When I'd finished, he lifted a skeleton hand and he pointed. Do you know what he pointed at?'

Jo shook her head.

'A flower,' said the Doctor softly. 'One of those little weeds. Just like a daisy it was. I looked at it for a moment, and suddenly I saw it through his eyes. It was simply glowing with life like a perfectly cut jewel, and the colours were deeper and richer than you could possibly imagine. It was the *daisiest* daisy I'd ever seen.'

'And that was the secret of life? A daisy?' She laughed. 'Honestly, Doctor!'

The Doctor smiled. 'Yes, I laughed too! Later, I got up and ran down that mountain and I found that the rocks weren't grey at all. They were red and brown and purple and gold. And those pathetic little patches of sludgy snow were shining white in the sunlight!'

The Doctor was silent for a moment or two. Then he said, 'Are you still frightened, Jo?'

'Not as much as I was.'

'I'm sorry I brought you here.'

'I'm not.'

'Thank you,' said the Doctor quietly.

Suddenly the cell door crashed open and a guard thrust Dalios into the cell. 'Inside, old man.'

Dalios made a quavering attempt to assert his dignity. 'I demand to be taken to the Queen.'

'You'll do as you're told,' said the guard indifferently, shoving him back.

Dalios was outraged. 'How dare you lay your hands on me? I *shall* see the Queen. Out of my way, slave.'

He tried to thrust the guard aside, and the guard, almost by reflex, swung the butt of his trident. Dalios staggered back beneath the blow and collapsed close to the Doctor and Jo. The guard moved away, slamming and locking the cell door.

By stretching their chains, the Doctor and Jo could just reach Dalios. The Doctor lifted the old man's head. 'Dalios!'

The old man had been badly beaten. The guard's blow was the last of many. His eyes fluttered. 'Who would have thought it – my sweet Queen . . .'

'Is the Master responsible for this?'

'Aye. He sought to bend me to his will . . . But it is no matter. Come closer . . . I have so little time . . .'

'What is it?' asked the Doctor gently.

Dalios's voice was faint. 'Atlantis is doomed. I tell you the vision of a dying man. You are a true philosopher, friend Doctor. The world must be saved . . . and you are the one to save it.' Dalios's head fell back, and his eyes closed.

'Don't worry, Dalios. We shan't fail you,' said the Doctor fiercely.

But Dalios could no longer hear him.

15

The Return of Kronos

Once again the Council of Atlantis was assembled in the great hall of the temple.

Once again, two figures sat on the throne-like seats on the raised stone. Just as before, one was Queen Galleia. But this time, the other was the Master.

Crito rapped on the floor with his staff of office. 'Silence. The Lady Galleia, Queen of Atlantis, speaks!'

Galleia rose. 'Brethren of the Council – my faithful few.' (This was a reference to the fact that over half the council had mysteriously disappeared.) In a ringing voice she continued: 'Our troubles are now at an end. No longer shall we fret beneath an old, defeated King. I present to you his Holiness, the Most Venerable Lord Master.'

The Master rose, looking about him with arrogant self-satisfaction. Everything was prepared.

In front of his own TARDIS stood the TOMTIT apparatus on a specially prepared altar, this time with the large crystal attached. Nearby sat the Doctor, a bound and guarded prisoner, with Jo at his side, unbound, and Krasis standing guard over her.

The Doctor looked up at the Master, standing on

the dais beside Galleia. 'Getting a bit above yourself, aren't you?'

'Silence!' screamed Krasis.

The Master began to speak. 'Greetings to you, my brothers. I grieve to see the Council so small. Yes I rejoice that you, the few who put me here have come to claim your just reward. You shall see the Mighty One himself, Kronos the Most Terrible.'

There was a murmur of awe from the little crowd.

The Master held up his hand, 'Krasis, the High Priest, will assist me. Krasis, beware!'

Krasis went to the TOMTIT console and operated the few simple controls that the Master had shown him the night before. There was a hum of power and the crowd drew back.

The Doctor raised his voice. 'What's happened to the rest of the Council? Are they alive?'

The Master looked down. 'The point is academic, Doctor. In another minute or so it will be of no further interest to you.'

'Satisfy my curiosity then. Are they indeed alive? Or are they dead – like King Dalios?'

'Dalios is unharmed,' said Galleia quickly.

'The King is dead, Madam,' said the Doctor.

'It's true,' said Jo. 'We were there in the cell with him when he died.'

Galleia stared at her. 'You were there? You saw him die?' She turned to the Master. 'Is this true?'

The Master made no answer.

Galleia rose and approached him. 'Is this true? Is the Lord Dalios, the King, no longer alive? *Answer me*!'

'He is dead,' said the Master indifferently.

'You were responsible for his death,' shouted the Doctor.

Galleia looked accusingly at the Master. 'But you promised me . . .'

'I promised you power,' said the Master impatiently. 'And you shall have it. Power to realise your most ambitious dreams.'

Galleia was not listening. 'You promised he should not be harmed.'

The Master shrugged. 'He was an old man – and stubborn.'

Galleia aimed a savage blow at his face, but he swept her hand aside and she fell back. She turned to the temple guards. 'Seize this man!'

As the guards began closing in on the Master, he called out: 'Krasis! The switch!'

'No! Stop him!' shouted the Doctor.

But it was too late.

Krasis threw the power switch and the Crystal blazed into fiery life.

The towering winged figure of Kronos seemed to burst from the heart of the Great Crystal, filling the temple with the beat of his mighty wings.

To his horror, the Doctor saw that in this manifestation Kronos was larger and more uncontrollable than ever – a fact that the Master failed to realise.

'I, the Master, welcome you Kronos,' he bellowed. 'I bid you to do my will.'

Kronos began swirling to and fro, swinging back and forth across the temple, sending the crowd fleeing in terror.

'Do you hear me, Kronos?' shouted the Master. He pointed to the Doctor. 'I command you to destroy that man!'

Kronos ignored him. Already the temple was beginning to shake, great stone blocks falling from the walls and ceiling. The air was filled with dust and the screams of the wounded and dying. There would be death and destruction in plenty in Atlantis that day, but it would be at the whim of Kronos alone.

'He'll never obey you,' shouted the Doctor. 'Don't you understand what you've done? He's uncontrollable.'

Even now the Master refused to admit defeat. 'I need more power,' he muttered. 'All the power in the Universe is waiting for me – in another time, another place.'

He ran to the TOMTIT apparatus and wrenched free the Great Crystal.

'Stop him,' shouted the Doctor. 'He mustn't get away!'

But no-one dared approach the Master or the Crystal.

No-one but Jo Grant.

Darting from her place at the Doctor's side Jo ran to the Master, reaching him just as the Crystal came free. In a desperate attempt to slow the Master down, she leaped upon his back.

It had not the slightest effect. The Master ran for his TARDIS clutching the Crystal, and carrying Jo Grant, who hung on like a child playing piggy-back.

To the Doctor's dismay, Jo, the Master and the Crystal all disappeared inside the Master's TARDIS – which promptly dematerialised.

The Doctor called to Galleia. 'Your Majesty, set me free!'

Galleia snatched a sword from the body of a fallen guard and began severing the Doctor's bonds. 'You and Dalios were right, Doctor,' she sobbed. 'I was wrong. Go quickly! It is too late now to save my people.'

The Doctor sprinted to his TARDIS and vanished inside. Moments later, the TARDIS too disappeared.

Queen Galleia stood alone in the centre of the temple. Above her Kronos roared to and fro, bringing down the roof and walls with his fiery passage, in an orgy of destruction.

The destruction would not come to an end until the entire city of Atlantis had been destroyed.

The Master was handcuffing Jo to the console of his TARDIS. (Just like the Master to have built-in fittings for prisoners, thought Jo.)

'There, Miss Grant. I think we've seen the last of the Doctor. Buried for all time under the ruins of Atlantis. You know, I'm going to miss him!'

'He's not finished,' said Jo stubbornly. 'I know it.'

'Nonsense, my dear. Of course he is.'

'You're the one who's finished,' said Jo. 'Do you really think that – thing out there will ever let you control it?'

'I do so already. He came at my call. You saw that for yourself.'

'Like a tiger comes when it hears a lamb bleating,' said Jo scornfully.

The Master smiled. 'Nicely put, my dear. Worthy of the late lamented Doctor himself.' He laughed exultantly. 'You know, I could kick myself for not having polished him off long ago.' He strolled over to the Great Crystal, which rested on a table by the console. 'Just think of the future. Dominion over all time and all space. Absolute power forever, and no Doctor to ruin things for me.'

'Don't worry, Jo,' said the Doctor's cheerful voice. 'I'll soon sort him out for you.'

Jo looked up and saw the Doctor's face beaming at her from the scanner screen. 'Doctor!'

The Master laughed, slightly bitterly this time. 'Really, Doctor, you must be as indestructible as that wretched TARDIS of yours! And how exactly do you propose to sort me out?'

'By making you see reason – and by making you destroy that Crystal.'

'And why should I do that? I have my TARDIS, I have Kronos, and I have Miss Grant. Now, my reason tells me that I hold all the cards.'

'But there's one you've forgotten,' said the Doctor calmly. 'I hold the trump card. I can stop you whenever I please.'

For a moment the Master looked worried, then he laughed. 'You're bluffing, Doctor.'

'Am I? What about Time Ram?'

'Time Ram,' said the Master uneasily. 'You couldn't do it in that pathetic old crock of yours. You'd never be able to lock on to my TARDIS.'

'I've already done it. The two TARDISes are operating on the same frequency, and our controls are locked together. See for yourself.'

To his horror the Master saw the needle on a particular dial creeping remorselessly towards the danger zone. 'You know what'll happen if that control goes over the safety limit, don't you? Tell him, Jo.'

A little unsteadily Jo said, 'The two TARDISes will occupy precisely the same space and the same time and that means –'

The Master slammed a fist down on the console. 'I know what it means!'

'Do you?' said the Doctor remorselessly.

The word seemed forced from the Master's lips. 'Oblivion.'

'Top of the class,' said the Doctor. 'Utter destruction. For you, the TARDIS, the Crystal.'

'And for you and your TARDIS and Miss Grant, Doctor,' snarled the Master.

'Of course. But Kronos will be free again, and the Universe saved.'

Defiantly the Master straightened up. 'Very well. Go ahead. Time Ram!'

'You don't mean it,' whispered Jo.

'Why should I dance to the Doctor's tune like a performing poodle. If you want to stop me, Doctor – *try*!'

'Very well,' said the Doctor quietly. 'Goodbye, Jo.'

'Goodbye, Doctor.'

The needle on the Master's dial crept closer and closer to the danger zone. It was hovering on the edge of it when it quivered and stopped.

The Master looked up at the screen. 'Well, Doctor, why have you stopped?'

'To give you one last chance.'

'Rubbish. You can't bring yourself to destroy Miss Grant. Admit it. It's that fatal weakness of yours, Doctor. Pity. Compassion.'

The Master pronounced the words like curses. 'For a moment, you almost had me believing you.'

'Don't think about me, Doctor,' called Jo. 'Think about the millions who will die. The millions who will never be born. Do it, Doctor, quickly!'

The Doctor hesitated. 'There may be another way, Jo.'

'Of course there is,' shouted the Master. 'The way to unimaginable glory.'

144

Jo saw that she could just reach the control on the Master's console – the equivalent control to the one the Doctor was using on his own. If she pulled that lever, it would mean Time Ram. Suddenly Jo Grant saw that she had to make the sacrifice that the Doctor would never make himself.

'Goodbye, Doctor!' She lunged forward and pulled the lever.

The needle slipped into the red zone.

Somewhere in space-time two TARDISes merged and disappeared. And for Jo Grant everything vanished in a ball of fiery white light.

Jo awoke to find herself, lying on the floor of the Master's TARDIS. Mysteriously, she had been freed from her handcuffs. Close by was the Master, stretched out unconscious.

Jo cautiously got to her feet, and made for the door. She opened it upon nothingness. Not land or sea or space – just nothingness.

Suspended in the nothingness, quite close, was the Doctor's TARDIS.

Jo stepped out into the void, walked carefully across to the police box and went inside.

The Doctor lay unconscious on the floor of the control room. Jo knelt beside him and shook him gently. 'Doctor. Wake up!'

He opened his eyes and blinked at her. 'Jo! Are you all right?'

'Oh yes,' said Jo, matter of factly. 'I'm dead, of course, but I'm all right.'

The Doctor got up. 'What on Earth are you talking about, Jo? You're no more dead than I am.'

'Yes, but that's it. I mean, that's what I *mean*. You're dead too – and so's the Master.'

'And I suppose we're in Heaven?'

Jo shrugged. 'Must be. Or somewhere. Come and have a look.'

She led the way to the still open door, and stepped out into the void. Cautiously the Doctor followed.

She turned to him, gesturing around the vast nothingness. 'Fantastic, isn't it?'

'Fascinating,' said the Doctor dryly. 'Though somehow I don't think we're in Heaven.'

'Well, where are we then?'

'That's just it,' admitted the Doctor. 'I don't know myself. You shouldn't have put us into Time Ram, Jo. Besides, I was just on the point of doing it myself.'

'Really?'

'Now look here, Jo –' He broke off, and smiled ruefully. 'No, not really.'

A sort of vast throat-clearing took place behind them and they turned to see a colossal face. It was a female face, beautiful and exotic, so large that they could have crawled upon the shapely nose like flies.

The Doctor was in a state where he felt nothing could surprise him. 'Greetings,' he said calmly.

The face spoke in a clear bell-like voice that reverberated everywhere. 'Your courtesy is always so punctilious, Doctor!'

'You know me?'

'Of old.'

'Do please forgive me, but I can't seem to place you.'

'I am Kronos,' said the face.

'You!' said Jo in amazement. 'But – you're a girl.'

'Shapes mean nothing.'

'But you were a raging monster before,' persisted Jo. 'An evil destroyer.'

'I can be all things,' said the voice. 'A destroyer, a healer, a creator. I am beyond good and evil as you know it.'

'Where exactly are we?' asked the Doctor.

'On the boundary of your reality and mine. You brought yourselves here.'

'With the Time Ram?'

'At the moment of impact I was released. That saved you . . . and took you here, to the threshold of being.'

The Doctor nodded. 'I see. So what happens now?'

'I owe you a debt of gratitude that nothing could repay. What would you wish?'

It was Jo who answered. 'To go back home.'

'In the TARDIS,' added the Doctor.

'You shall.'

'What about the Master?' asked Jo curiously.

'He will stay here.'

'What will happen to him?'

'Torment,' said the face sweetly. 'The pain he has given so freely shall be returned to him in full.'

The Master staggered out from his TARDIS and fell to his knees. 'No,' he screamed. 'Please Doctor, help me. I can't bear it. Please, Doctor, please!'

The Doctor turned back to the great face. 'O mighty Kronos, I ask one more favour of you.'

'Name it.'

'The Master's freedom.'

'He made a prisoner of me!' said the voice angrily.

'I know. But will you allow us to deal with him in our way?'

147

'I do not understand you. But if that is your desire, so let it be.'

The Master rose from his knees and stood facing the Doctor. 'Thank you, Doctor,' he said humbly.

'Don't thank me,' said the Doctor brusquely. 'You're coming back to Earth with us.'

The Master bowed his head, clearly a broken man. 'Yes, of course,' he whispered.

The Doctor stepped back and motioned the Master to enter the TARDIS. The Master walked slowly forward, gave the Doctor a shove that sent him staggering against Jo, spun round and vanished inside his own TARDIS.

'Stop him,' yelled the Doctor, but it was too late.

The Master's TARDIS promptly dematerialised.

'You asked for him to be given his freedom,' said the voice amusedly. 'He has it!'

'Here we go again,' said Jo.

She followed the Doctor into his TARDIS.

Stuart Hyde held out a spoonful of mush to the baby on the laboratory floor. It stared disapprovingly at the spoon and said distinctly, 'No!'

'Come on, Baby Benton,' coaxed Stuart. 'Come on, get it down you!'

Ruth looked up from her work at the console. 'What are you feeding him on now?'

'The remains of my lunchtime sandwiches, mashed up with some cold tea.'

'Well, stop playing mothers and fathers and come and give me a hand here. I think I'm nearly there.'

'What are you trying to do?'

'Well, if I'm on the beam, I should be able to close up the gap in time for good,' She made a last adjustment. 'Right, switch on, Stu.'

'Okay!' Putting down his saucer of improvised baby food, Stuart switched on.

Inside the TARDIS, Jo was saying, 'But why, Doctor? Why did you even ask?'

The Doctor adjusted the controls, and studied the rise and fall of the central column.

'Would you condemn anybody to an eternity of torment, Jo – even the Master?'

'No, I suppose I wouldn't.'

'Well, neither would I – even if he was responsible for the destruction of Atlantis.'

'It's terrible when you think of it,' said Jo suddenly. 'All those people . . .'

The central column was slowing its rise and fall.

'Jo,' said the Doctor gently, 'we're about to land in England – in your time. That all happened three thousand five hundred years ago . . .'

Once again Stuart was calling out the readings, 'Three five, four zero . . .'

'Increasing power,' said Ruth.

Suddenly another sound drowned out the TOMTIT noise, and a blue police box appeared in a corner of the lab. The Doctor and Jo Grant stepped out.

'Suffering monkeys!' said Stuart faintly.

Ruth was too absorbed in her experiment to notice. 'Now concentrate, Stu!' she called. 'Isolate matrix scanner.'

'Check!' He returned to the power readings. 'Six zero, six five, seven zero . . .'

'See if it's working, Stu!'

Stuart ran to the window and saw that the Brigadier and his men were back to normal. He could hear the Brigadier shouting orders.

Stuart turned back from the window. 'Yes, it is!'

'Good!'

The Doctor studied the power readings. 'It seems to be working a bit too well.'

'It's running away,' shouted Ruth.

'Everybody get down!' shouted Stu. 'It's going to go up!'

They all took cover as the TOMTIT console overloaded and blew up.

In the absence of the crystal however, the result was nothing more serious than a loud bang, a shower of sparks and a lot of smoke.

Ruth got to her feet and studied the shattered console.

'You'll have to start all over again,' said Jo.

Ruth shook her head. 'I couldn't, not without the Professor. Just as well I suppose.'

'Well, it's done its job, thanks to you,' said the Doctor. 'Everything's back to normal.'

As if to prove the Doctor's point, the Brigadier burst into the room, revolver in hand. 'Stand quite still everyone.' He broke off, staring round the somewhat unexpected group. 'Er – where's the Master?'

'A very good question, Brigadier,' said the Doctor.

'Ah, Doctor, glad to see you're back. And you Miss Grant . . .'

The Brigadier suddenly registered Jo's Atlantean costume. 'Miss Grant, what are you doing in that extraordinary get-up?' Without waiting for a reply the Brigadier went on, 'And where, for heaven's sake, is Sergeant Benton?'

Stuart clutched Ruth's arm. 'The baby! We forgot the baby!'

Sergeant Benton arose from behind the TOMTIT console. He had been restored to his full age and size, and he was wearing nothing but a very inadequate improvised nappy, and an embarrassed smile.

He looked around the circle of smiling faces, and said plaintively. 'Would someone please tell me exactly what's been happening around here?'

And that too, thought the Doctor, was a very good question!

DOCTOR WHO

0426114558	TERRANCE DICKS **Doctor Who and The Abominable Snowmen**	£1.35
0426200373	**Doctor Who and The Android Invasion**	£1.25
0426201086	**Doctor Who and The Androids of Tara**	£1.35
0426116313	IAN MARTER **Doctor Who and The Ark in Space**	£1.35
0426201043	TERRANCE DICKS **Doctor Who and The Armageddon Factor**	£1.50
0426112954	**Doctor Who and The Auton Invasion**	£1.50
0426116747	**Doctor Who and The Brain of Morbius**	£1.35
0426110250	**Doctor Who and The Carnival of Monsters**	£1.35
042611471X	MALCOLM HULKE **Doctor Who and The Cave Monsters**	£1.50
0426117034	TERRANCE DICKS **Doctor Who and The Claws of Axos**	£1.35
042620123X	DAVID FISHER **Doctor Who and The Creature from the Pit**	£1.35
0426113160	DAVID WHITAKER **Doctor Who and The Crusaders**	£1.50
0426200616	BRIAN HAYLES **Doctor Who and The Curse of Peladon**	£1.50
0426114639	GERRY DAVIS **Doctor Who and The Cybermen**	£1.50
0426113322	BARRY LETTS **Doctor Who and The Daemons**	£1.50

Prices are subject to alteration

STAR Books are obtainable from many booksellers and newsagents. If you have any difficulty please send purchase price plus postage on the scale below to:

> **Star Cash Sales**
> **P.O. Box 11**
> **Falmouth**
> **Cornwall**
> OR
> **Star Book Service,**
> **G.P.O. Box 29,**
> **Douglas,**
> **Isle of Man,**
> **British Isles.**

While every effort is made to keep prices low, it is sometimes necessary to increase prices at short notice. Star Books reserve the right to show new retail prices on covers which may differ from those advertised in the text or elsewhere.

Postage and Packing Rate

UK: 55p for the first book, 22p for the second book and 14p for each additional book ordered to a maximum charge of £1.75p. BFPO and EIRE: 55p for the first book, 22p for the second book, 14p per copy for the next 7 books, thereafter 8p per book. Overseas: £1.00p for the first book and 25p per copy for each additional book.

THIS OFFER EXCLUSIVE TO

READERS

Pin up magnificent full colour posters of DOCTOR WHO

Just send £2.50 for the first poster and £1.25 for each additional poster

TO: PUBLICITY DEPARTMENT *
W. H. ALLEN & CO PLC
44 HILL STREET
LONDON W1X 8LB

Cheques, Postal Orders made payable to WH Allen PLC

POSTER 1 ☐   **POSTER 2** ☐   **POSTER 3** ☐
POSTER 4 ☐   **POSTER 5** ☐

Please allow 28 DAYS for delivery.

I enclose £ _____

CHEQUE NO. _____

ACCESS, VISA CARD NO. _____

Name _____

Address _____

_____

_____

*** For Australia, New Zealand, USA and Canada apply to distributors
listed on back cover for details and local price list**